# PUERTO RICO

# BOOKS BY DENIS J. HAUPTLY

The Journey from the Past
In Vietnam
A Convention of Delegates
Puerto Rico: An Unfinished Story

# PUERTO RICO

## An Unfinished Story

## Denis J. Hauptly

Atheneum 1991 New York

COLLIER MACMILLAN CANADA   Toronto
MAXWELL MACMILLAN INTERNATIONAL PUBLISHING GROUP
New York   Oxford   Singapore   Sydney

*J 972.95*
*H*

*753/92*

# ACKNOWLEDGMENTS

*This book has benefited from a number of conversations over the years with friends from Puerto Rico, which both sparked my interest and provided varied perspectives on the island and its history. In addition, and in particular, I gratefully acknowledge the comments and criticisms of Judge José A. Cabranes of the United States District Court for the District of Connecticut, who provided both written and oral commentary on the manuscript. He has saved me from many errors but bears no responsibility for those that may remain.*

Copyright © 1991 by Denis J. Hauptly

Atheneum
Macmillan Publishing Company
866 Third Avenue
New York, NY 10022

Collier Macmillan Canada, Inc.
1200 Eglinton Avenue East
Suite 200
Don Mills, Ontario M3C 3N1

First edition
Printed in the United States of America
1  2  3  4  5  6  7  8  9  10
Designed by Kimberly M. Hauck

Library of Congress Cataloging-in-Publication Data
Hauptly, Denis J.
Puerto Rico: an unfinished story/by Denis J. Hauptly.—1st ed.
p.    cm.
Includes bibliographical references and index.
Summary: Examines the history, culture, society, and future of this beautiful island in the Caribbean Sea.
ISBN 0-689-31431-0
1. Puerto Rico—History—Juvenile literature. [1. Puerto Rico—History.] I. Title.
F1971.H4 1991
972.95—dc20 90-37953  CIP  AC

Prints and photographs courtesy of the National Archives

*To Kay A. Knapp,*
*whose patience*
*and care have made*
*this book, and much*
*else, possible*

# Contents

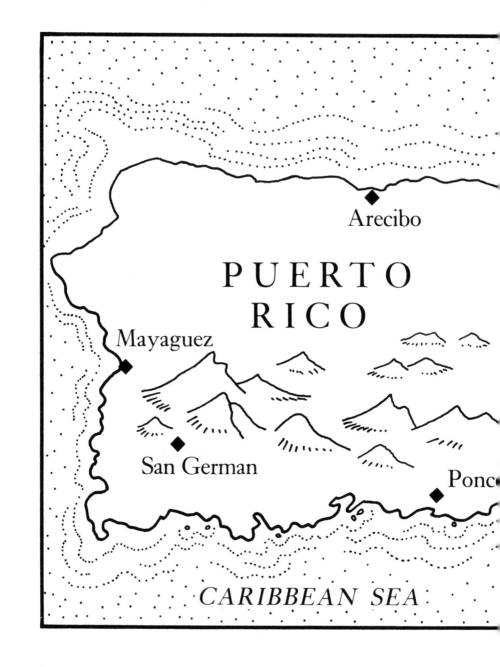

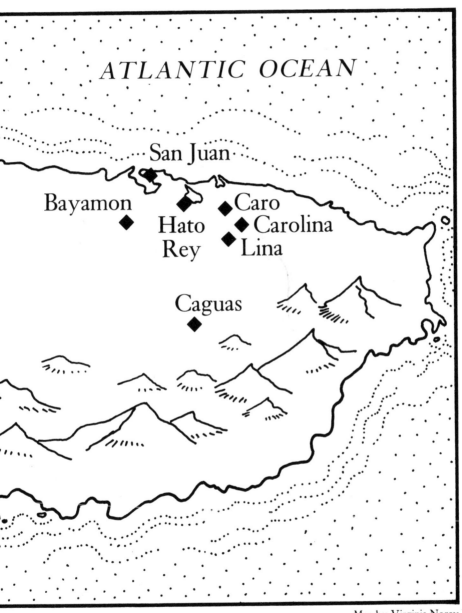

ATLANTIC OCEAN

San Juan

Bayamon

Caro

Hato Rey

Carolina

Lina

Caguas

Map by Virginia Norey

# Introduction

*Puerto Rico is a land of double meanings. It is a Spanish* culture under American rule. It is Old World and it is Third World. It is the oldest European settlement in the New World, but it was among the last areas to be settled by early native American people. Its residents are American citizens, but it is not a part of the United States. Its people are united in their deep love for their island and its culture, but as deeply divided in their views as to that island's future.

Will Puerto Rico tie itself permanently to the United States by becoming a state? Will it sever all ties with the mainland and become an independent nation? Will it maintain its present course, a separate culture with strong political and economic ties to the United States?

In exploring Puerto Rico and its rich culture and history, we must try to think as people living on that island. Any other view will lead us to false conclusions. If we see Puerto Rico from the viewpoint of mainland Americans, we will imagine that Puerto Ricans are just like us in

*1*

every way. We will think that they share the same history, the same society, and the same future. But Puerto Rican history is quite different from mainland history. Puerto Rican society is quite different from mainland society. And Puerto Rico's future is the subject of a debate that has gone on for half a century and is not likely to be resolved in this century.

How do we gain the viewpoint of a Puerto Rican if we are not Puerto Rican? First, and most difficult, we forget everything we have ever thought about Puerto Rico except those things that we have learned from Puerto Ricans themselves. Even then we must be careful, because things that we may have learned from Puerto Ricans who have lived on the mainland for long may be filtered through an American eye. But if we have seen art from Puerto Rico or heard Puerto Ricans talk about life in their neighborhoods or towns, we can keep those memories.

Second, we must go back to the very beginning. We cannot walk into modern San Juan and understand the culture of Puerto Rico. The society we see today is a mixture. There are some parts that represent Spanish culture, the language and much of the architecture and literature, for instance. There are some parts that represent American culture, such as the goods for sale or the form of government.

If we go back to the beginning, we will be able to understand which parts of this complex society are deeply rooted and which are newly planted. We will then be able to think about which of the newly planted parts are likely to take root and become a permanent part of Puerto Rican culture and which of the deeply rooted parts have grown old and are dying. We may not be able to decide for certain what tomorrow will look like in Puerto Rico, but we will be able to understand better how things have become the way they are today.

Throughout all of this, we should keep in mind that it is the Puerto Rican people who will decide their own future. Their decision will be based on their judgment as to what is best for Puerto Rico. The decision is a very difficult one because whatever choice is made involves some deep sacrifice. If Puerto Ricans choose independence, then they will lose the security and prestige that comes from ties with the world's most powerful nation. If they choose statehood, then they risk the loss of their culture as the island becomes increasingly Americanized. If they maintain their present commonwealth status, then the debate that has divided the island will continue. The question of Puerto Rico's future is called the status question, and there are no easy answers to it.

For the moment, let us look at the things that we can know for sure, the past, and let us begin at the very beginning, before European women and men made their dangerous way to that beautiful island in the Caribbean.

# 1

# Before Columbus

*Millions of years before time was measured, the land we now* know as Puerto Rico was a part of the huge land mass that geologists have blessed with the name Gondwanaland. It was wedged between what are now North America, South America, and Africa. Each of these, in turn, rested on a huge plate that formed a part of the earth's crust. Over thousands and millions of years, these plates drifted on the molten core of the earth, and the continents slowly took their present positions.

As North and South America drifted apart, part of that enormous mountain chain that runs from the Rockies through the Andes filled in the gap now occupied by the Isthmus of Panama. The base of the mountains was covered by the sea, and to the eye, they became islands. As more time passed, these islands floated eastward on their plate. They formed a near barrier between the tip of Florida and the northern coast of South America. This group of islands is called the Greater Antilles and is made up of Cuba, Jamaica, Puerto Rico, and Hispaniola (the island that contains both Haiti and the Dominican Republic). Extending past the Greater Antilles to South America are the Lesser Antilles, formed when the Caribbean plate pushed into the Atlantic plate.

The Greater Antilles were among the last places on earth to be lived in by humans. Millions of years after Africa was populated and tens of thousands of years after mankind had made its long journey to North and South America, these lovely islands remained empty. There were no voices; there were no homes. No one hunted in the forests; no one sailed on the seas.

But the land was alive with animals and plants, especially plants. These included corn and beans, peppers and squash—plants that thrived in the tropics and that needed no farmer to sow their seeds.

Behind these empty islands, to the north and to the south, the great continents of the New World lay empty too. The people of the earth were in Africa, Asia, and Europe. There they could hunt game and gather plants and live their lives. They had no great need to travel. The forests were vast, and the people were few.

But around twenty-five thousand years ago, some of these people, pushed by human curiosity and given the opportunity by the ending of the Ice Age, began to explore their world. They traveled through western Asia to the tip of what is now the Soviet Union. Today they would have found the Bering Sea and they might have stopped. But at that time, there was no Bering Sea. There was a strip of land, two hundred miles wide, that connected Asia with modern-day Alaska. This dry and frigid land is referred to as Beringia.

At some unknown time, but at least fifteen thousand

years ago, they crossed Beringia and entered North America. Eventually, they began to move south. When that happened exactly is a matter of some debate. It may have been twelve thousand years ago. There is one group of scientists who think that the whole movement from Asia may have happened one hundred thousand years ago.

Whenever the journey south began and by whatever route it was made, the new and warmer land that they came to gave them a new opportunity. Food was abundant, and space was unlimited. There was no great need to continue traveling. The only area that had not been explored was the ocean. These people were not sailors and had no idea what the ocean contained, so they did not venture out beyond the sight of land for many centuries. The Greater Antilles remained empty.

There may have been early visits from the mainland. Indians by then had populated much of North America, traveling across the Great Plains and the Southwest. The Indians were in Florida, and that is only ninety miles from Cuba. The native people on the northeast coast of South America could well have hopped along the Lesser Antilles to the Greater Antilles. The two island chains are set out like rocks across a stream. There are some pottery remains and other signs that visitors, called the Ciboney, stopped in Puerto Rico in ancient times. But there is no evidence of real settlements until about the time of Christ.

The first settlers were called the Arawaks. This is a general name given to a group of tribes that shared similar languages and cultures. They had come from an area around the mouth of the Orinoco River in what is now Venezuela. They had developed rafts, and even canoes, and had probably traveled first to Trinidad, a large island just off the coast of Venezuela. They probably began their journey along the island chains between 1000 and 500 B.C. Their first known settlement in Puerto Rico is at Loiza on the north coast. It dates back to A.D. 120.

The first group of Arawaks to arrive was called the Igneris. They named the island Boriquen, which means "the land of the brave lord." The Igneris probably did not farm, but gathered their food by hunting and fishing. Very little is known about them other than what their housing was like and what the pieces of pottery that have been found in the remains of their villages reveal. The pottery is of a very high quality and suggests a people who placed a high value on beauty.

We know about Arawak housing from Arawak settlements in other parts of Latin America. Their houses were round, with walls of saplings and with cone-shaped, thatched roofs. The saplings for the walls and the grasses for the roofs were readily available. Such housing would not be very sturdy, of course, but in the warm tropical climate of Boriquen, the chief purpose of housing was to keep people dry, and these houses were well suited for that purpose. They did not provide any protection against the great scourge of the Caribbean, the hurricane, though. These fierce tropical storms, with driving rain and winds over one hundred miles per hour, have always been a part of Caribbean life. As we shall see, they have had a great effect on the history of Puerto Rico.

By about A.D. 500, the Igneris had been replaced by another group of Arawaks called the Ostionoids. These people seem to have been more practical. The things that they left behind included many well-made tools. The Ostionoids were particularly skilled at working with stone. In addition to tools, they used polished stones to make religious objects of worship, showing a fairly advanced culture. They also moved inland from the coast, exploring and settling the interior of Boriquen. They built large plazas that were used for games and for religious ceremonies.

Around A.D. 1000, the Ostionoids were in turn replaced by the Tainos, a third Arawak group. Their name means "gentle." They were not only gentle, they were also skilled engineers and farmers, and a deeply religious people. They, like other Arawaks, had a language that was spoken throughout the island and could be understood on the mainland of South America. This common language and their skill as sailors allowed them to trade with the people of South and Central America. Theirs was not an isolated culture.

The Tainos slept in hammocks, a word that is taken from their word—*hamaca.* They were skilled bakers and expert boat makers. There was enough spare time in their society for artists to make paintings on stone and for complex legends to be passed on from generation to generation.

These were a people who could build a great civilization. Farming is a cooperative activity and it bonds people into groups and also keeps them in one place. As an

agricultural society, they also had a complex social structure. The *cacique* was the chieftain of the village, and the
village *caciques* were ruled over by sixteen regional
*caciques* who served under an island *cacique*. Under the
village *caciques* were the *nitainos,* or nobles of the village.
The lowest class in this society were the workers, who
were called *naborias.*

The chief god of the Tainos was named *Yocahu*. The
god of the ferocious winds was called *Juracan*. If you
pronounce that name as though the first letter were an
*H*, you would hear a word like our *hurricane*. Weather,
in particular the deadly hurricanes that haunt the Caribbean, was a major factor in the lives of the Tainos.

In the center of each village was a plaza, often paved,
called a *batey*. Here the Tainos met for public meetings,
dances, funerals, and other religious ceremonies. Like the
other Indians in South and Central America, the Tainos
also used these plazas for a game played with a rubberlike
ball. The game appears to have been as much a religious
event as an athletic one.

It is very important to realize that these were not primitive people. This was an advanced society. It is true they
had no guns and they had not invented printing. They
had not built large cities. But they were not far behind the
European culture as history measures time. The Tainos
may not have been as advanced as the Incas and the Mayas
on the mainland. They were more like the pioneers in the
western United States in the 1800s. They had given up
some of the comforts of the main society in order to
explore and tame new lands.

The Tainos were a peaceful people. But not all of the people of the Caribbean were peaceful. After the Arawaks had traveled through the Lesser Antilles, they were followed by the Caribs. The Caribs come down to us through history, Spanish history, as an incredibly fierce people. Their name is the source of the word *Caribbean* as well as the word *cannibal.* There is some evidence to suggest that they did engage in cannibalism as a ritual after a victory in battle.

Whether they were cannibals or not, they were certainly warriors. It seems that a great deal of their culture was based on war, on conquering other peoples. By the 1400s, the Caribs had begun to raid the Taino towns in the Greater Antilles. While the Tainos remained in control of Boriquen until the coming of the Europeans, their hold on the eastern part of the island had greatly weakened.

This, then, is how it was in Puerto Rico when the Europeans arrived. A peaceful and growing culture with a population of thirty thousand to seventy thousand people had been set up, a civilization on the brink of becoming an important one. It was under attack from a less advanced culture, but it was holding its own.

The Tainos might have succeeded in winning this war, but we will never know. A new group of invaders soon came upon them. At first, they tried to deal with these newcomers, and then they tried to fight them off. But their bows and arrows and spears were no match for the guns and cannon of the Spaniards. And no weapon of the time could fight the new diseases that the Spanish brought with them. In a matter of a few decades, most of the Taino were gone. Indeed, only a small trace of the entire Arawak nation remains today. Their sad story would be repeated in the French and English colonies to the north.

# 2

# The European Discovery

*Columbus was not the first European to come to the New* World, though his role was very important. No one will ever know for sure who that first person was. But the evidence and logic support the idea that the first Europeans in the Americas were Vikings.

Archaeologists have found a Viking settlement at a place called L'Anse aux Meadows at the very northern tip of Newfoundland, Canada. The settlement dates back to around A.D. 1000. It, and others like it, may have been fishing or hunting camps, used only part of the year, or they may have been an effort to start permanent colonies. Whatever they were, the Viking settlements disappeared over time, and the few Europeans who had had some knowledge of the New World were ignored for centuries.

Europe was emerging from the Dark Ages and was dividing up into the nations that are familiar to us today. It was also fighting off a challenge from the Moslems, who had invaded from the Middle East in the eighth century and who were not driven out until the end of the fifteenth century. Europeans, even Vikings, had little time to explore the oceans or a strange New World.

By the late 1400s, though, the last of the Moslem invaders had been driven out of Europe. The Crusades, fought between the eleventh and fifteenth centuries, had given Europeans a taste of the riches of Asia, and European sailors had found their way around Africa to India. The African route was a long and difficult one, though, and land travel to Asia was even longer and more dangerous because one had to travel through hostile Moslem territory.

Europeans knew that the world was round. Only the very ignorant believed that it was flat. Since they knew that the world was round, they also knew that if they could get to India by sailing east around Africa, they could also get there by sailing west into the Atlantic Ocean, unless there was something like a continent to block their path.

But they did not believe that there was a continent in their way. For one thing, they had never heard of such a continent, so they had no reason to imagine it. For another thing, many believed in mathematical estimates of the size of the globe that were way off. They may have believed that the earth was much smaller than it actually is. By their calculations, there was no room on the globe for anything other than Europe, Africa, and Asia. Others used more accurate measurements. They knew about how large the earth really is, but they still had no strong reason for believing that a vast land mass stood between them and Asia.

It is one thing to believe that you can reach Asia by

sailing west and quite another thing to get into a small boat, sail off into uncharted seas, and look for it. That takes great navigational skill and even greater courage. The Europeans were skilled seamen, but even their great voyages around the tip of Africa to India had been in sight of land. They did not have to figure out where they were; they could look and see the coast of Africa or know that it was just a few miles off. If a storm came, they could head for the coast to take shelter.

Christopher Columbus had both the skills and the courage. Very little is known of the early life of the most famous sailor in history. It seems certain that he was born in Genoa, Italy, and that his birth took place in 1451. His father was a weaver, and two of his brothers, Bartholomew, and Diego assisted on some of his voyages.

He had probably gone to sea when he was quite young. Italy was not a unified nation at that time, and he would have sailed for whatever nation seemed the most attractive. In 1476, he was on board an Italian vessel that was attacked by a French ship. Columbus's ship caught fire, and he swam to the coast of Portugal.

Apparently the swim was a dangerous one, for Columbus took his safe arrival on Portuguese soil as a sign. He committed himself to Portugal and, in the plans he was to develop over the next few years, he imagined himself sailing under a Portuguese flag.

Again the record is unclear, but it appears that Columbus did sail for Portugal for a number of years and that he went as far as Iceland and the West African coast. In both of these places, he must have heard tales, true or untrue, of a land to the west. He himself became absolutely sure that Asia was only a few weeks' sail to the west.

He had married a prominent Portuguese woman and, through her, he was able to present his plan to the Portuguese king. But the king was doubtful, and another Portuguese navigator, Bartholomew Dias, had just reported back from his successful trip around the tip of Africa. Even if there was a western route, there was no need to look for it so long as there was an eastern one.

But Columbus was a driven man. He was driven by the challenge of finding the western route. He was driven by the idea that his views were correct and should be tested. He was driven by a desire for fame and riches. If Portugal would not sponsor his trip, he would try Spain.

He spent six years of his life in an effort to convince the Spanish rulers to finance his scheme. They really didn't need too much convincing. Spain was way behind the Portuguese in trade, and it wanted to catch up and pull ahead. But the Moslem invaders still had a grip in Spain, and they had to be taken care of first. In January of 1492, the last battle against the Moslems was fought, and finally Ferdinand and Isabella, the king and queen of Spain, agreed to sponsor Columbus.

He was given three ships, the largest of which by far, the *Santa María,* was only 115 feet long. On August 3, 1492, he set out from Spain and made his way to the Canary Islands off the coast of Africa. From there, on September 6, he sailed west. Or he tried to sail west. His little ships were at the mercy of the waves and the currents, and his compasses were not very accurate, so the route he actually took was southwest. Even that route was changed a little by a false sighting of land on September 25.

On the morning of October 12, 1492, Columbus did indeed sight land. There has been a long dispute about what island it was that he first saw and landed at. For a long time, the little island of San Salvador, or Watling Island, was believed to be the landfall. Recent computer analyses make a very strong case for an island to the south of San Salvador, between Cuba and Hispaniola, called Samana Cay. Not only does that island fit the track that the computers predict, given the winds and the currents, but also its physical characteristics match up with those described by Columbus.

After spending several days on Samana Cay, Columbus took several islanders with him and set out to explore other islands in the area. He visited the Bahamas and Cuba and Hispaniola. Along the way, though, he lost one of his ships. The *Santa María* ran aground in Hispaniola and was destroyed.

Columbus left forty of his sailors on Hispaniola to set up a colony when he returned to Spain. They were never seen again.

Columbus arrived in Spain a hero and was almost immediately on his way back to the New World, which he always believed was Asia. This time, though, the voyage was to be one of settlement, not exploration. Columbus commanded a fleet of seventeen ships with more than 1,200 men aboard. He reached the Caribbean again on

November 3, 1493, coasted from island to island, and landed in Puerto Rico on November 19. He gave the island the name of San Juan Bautista, Saint John the Baptist.

After exploring the island briefly, he returned to Hispaniola, where he had left his sailors ten months before. There he found that his men had so upset the Tainos with their greed for gold that the *cacique* Caonabo had killed them and destroyed their little colony. Columbus set up another colony, but it too ran into trouble. The Spanish wanted gold, and the island did not have any, nor did the natives think much of it. The land of Hispaniola was a good place for farming, not mining, and Columbus's men were not interested in being farmers.

After his efforts to force the nonexistent gold from the Indians had failed, Columbus set up a system of plantations. His sailors were given land and control of the Indians who lived on the land. The Indians became the slaves of the Spanish sailors. The product that they farmed on the plantations was sugar, which Columbus had brought with him on this voyage. For four and one-half centuries, this crop was to be a major force in the lives of the Puerto Ricans and the other people of the Caribbean. It would bring war to many and wealth to a few.

The Indians were not among those few who prospered from sugar. Under forced labor, harsh treatment, and faced with new diseases that their bodies could not fight off, the Indians began to die out. When Columbus arrived, there were three hundred thousand Indians on Hispaniola. Fifty years later, there were none.

The colony of Hispaniola became the base for Spanish exploration of what many, but not Columbus, believed to be a new world. Columbus returned to Spain, but found that his triumph was short-lived. He had come back with little gold and no profit. The Spanish court began to plot against him. Columbus was Italian, not Spanish. He had promised the riches of Asia, but he brought back parrots and bananas.

Nonetheless, Columbus and his voyage were famous enough to cause the Spanish rulers to provide him with a third fleet. He returned in 1498 and discovered the coast of South America. But his influence had faded. In 1499, Francesco de Bobadilla was sent to the new colonies to act as royal commissioner. He sent Columbus and his brothers back to Spain as prisoners. In 1501, Nicolas de Ovando was appointed governor of the new colonies, and he now had thousands of Spaniards at his command. With them, he began to colonize the Caribbean Islands.

In 1508, Juan Ponce de León, a former aide to Columbus, commanded Spanish troops in capturing the island Columbus had called San Juan, and three years later he established his capital at Villa Rica de Puerto Rico, now the city of San Juan. So what we now call Puerto Rico used to be called San Juan, and what we now call San Juan used to be called Puerto Rico. To keep things simple, from now on the modern names will be used. The island will be called Puerto Rico, and the city will be called San Juan.

When Ponce arrived, there were four major *caciques* on the island. The interior on the western part of the island was ruled by Guarionex. The center of the island was headed by Orocobix. The eastern interior's chief was Mabo, and Caguax controlled the eastern coastal area.

The first year or so of the Spanish presence on the island was peaceful. The Spanish were welcomed by the Tainos who, perhaps, saw them as allies against the Caribs. But the pattern set in Hispaniola was soon repeated in Puerto Rico. The Tainos were enslaved in a system that was called *rapartimiento.* Under this system, those Spaniards who were willing to settle in the new colonies were given land and the right to have the labor of the local Indians. In theory, these Indians were not slaves, but in fact they were forced to work for their new Spanish landlords. In 1511, the Tainos rebelled against the Spanish. They were led by the *caciques* Caguax and Guarionex, who had at least three thousand men fighting the Spanish. But the Spanish had brought something with them from Europe other than trinkets and disease. They had brought guns, and the Tainos were armed only with primitive weapons. They were no match for the Spanish, and the rebellion was crushed. The final defeat came at the end of the year at the town of Yagueca on the west coast.

The remaining Tainos spread out. Some joined the Caribs, who were fighting the Spanish along the east coast of Puerto Rico. Others continued to live in Spanish-controlled villages and gradually intermarried with the Spanish colonists. After slaves from Africa had joined the population, intermarriage included the Africans as well. Unlike the colonists in the North America, the Spanish settlers did not frown on intermarriage with Africans. Sometime after the 1511 rebellion, Caguax died and was replaced as *cacique* by his daughter Baganaame. Soon after, she married one of the Spanish leaders. Thus, the native culture of Puerto Rico gradually merged with and became lost in the new culture. Some small remnant of the original Taino culture remained in Puerto Rico until the late 1700s, and then it disappeared. As with many other of the South American Indian cultures, the Taino was lost forever.

It should be understood that the Spanish were not in Puerto Rico or South America to establish friendly relations. They were there to obtain wealth and power. In this, they were in great competition with Portugal. Shortly after Columbus's first voyage, the Portuguese had gone to the pope and asked him to divide up the New World so that the Spanish and the Portuguese would not fight over it. Since there was no real knowledge of the geography of the new land, the Portuguese received that part of South America, Brazil, that sticks out farther east then the rest of the New World. Spain received the rest.

The Spanish did not know how much land was theirs, and they knew that whatever the pope had given them, the French and the English would like to take away. Nations that were battling in the Old World were not likely to decide that the New World, with all of its hoped-for riches, was a neutral zone. From the very beginning, this New World was seen as a battleground that the strongest European countries would control.

From what the Spanish did know of their new territory, the Caribbean Islands were the military key. They controlled access to Central America and to the northern coast of South America. The Spanish did not care about the eastern coast, for that was Portuguese. And they did not know about the western coast, because no European had yet made the journey to the Pacific Ocean.

So they decided to make their fortress and their stand along the Greater and Lesser Antilles. The people whom they sent to populate these islands were not merchants and bankers. They were soldiers, and they were soldiers who were anxious to conquer as much as possible as quickly as possible because they wanted to become rich and famous.

Puerto Rico, Hispaniola, and Cuba were forts on the frontier. They were centers for the conquest of Mexico and of South and Central America. The native populations were obstacles to making those forts secure. That meant, from a military point of view, that the natives had to be pacified or they had to be eliminated. To understand that is not to excuse what happened. Hundreds of thousands and perhaps millions of the natives of the New World were to die in the next few decades. Most died from diseases that the conquerors did not deliberately bring to the natives. Many died in battle or in slavery. Many others became a part of the new community, adopting its religion and customs. Their cultures, rich and promising, were lost for all of time. That loss is one we will never be able fully to appreciate, because we do not know what these people would have contributed to our society. But even if we do not fully understand the nature of the loss, this wave of death and this vanished culture must be remembered with sorrow and with shame.

What the Spanish had taken by the force of arms, though, they would have to hold by the force of arms as well. As their explorations in Mexico and South America yielded the long-sought-after gold, the people and the nations who were interested in the simple colonies in the Caribbean increased.

The fabled Spanish galleons began their voyages from Spain to the New World and back in the early 1500s. While they were not all filled to the brim with gold, silver, and precious gems, an enormous amount of wealth was taken from the New World back to Spain. All of these ships stopped in Puerto Rico, whose great harbor at San Juan became the major port of call for the Spanish fleet.

At the same time as Puerto Rico and the rest of the Antilles were becoming important because of their strategic positions, they were actually losing their Spanish population. As mentioned before, their Spanish settlers were not interested in setting up shops. They were interested in gold and power, and it turned out that those could be found on the mainland, not on the islands.

Ponce de León himself left in 1512 on a voyage of discovery to Florida. He died after battle with the Indians there, never having found the Fountain of Youth that he sought.

The Spanish fleets and, eventually, the islands themselves began to come under attack. At first, these attacks were from solitary pirates roaming the seas in search of quick riches. They were serious, but they could be tolerated. It was not long, though, until the other nations of Europe sent fleets of well-equipped warships.

Such attacks threatened not only the loss of an occasional ship, but the entire Spanish empire in the New World. It was part of a larger struggle for supremacy then going on among the European powers. In itself, the battle in the Americas was not a very big deal, but as part of the larger struggle and as a struggle for the wealth needed to carry on the battle in Europe, it was quite important indeed.

This struggle would lead to the next phase in the history of Puerto Rico, that of an island fortress, defender of the Spanish empire in the far-off colonies.

# 3

# A Spanish Colony

*The New World was a world of promise to the Europeans. It* promised wealth, opportunity for fame, and a chance to be free from the difficulties of the Old World. But those difficulties would haunt the New World as well, and Puerto Rico in particular.

Europe in the 1500s was a continent in turmoil. The national boundaries now so familiar to us had only recently been formed, and there was still considerable dispute about which people controlled which area. Some modern nations, such as Germany and Italy, were still little more than collections of small states with a common language.

Religious differences had also become important. Before the 1500s, Europe was united in having only one religion—Catholicism—among the various languages and cultures. This religious unity provided more than just a common set of values. It also provided a single leader, the pope, who could command kings and princes. But the Reformation changed that; or perhaps the Reformation

*24*

was a visible sign that deeper and quieter changes had already taken place.

The union represented by the pope in Rome was always more apparent than real. An Italian religious figure is not a likely candidate to have final power in the faraway nations of northern Europe. As these countries reached maturity, as they became more like nations and less like tribes, the control of Rome and the religion of Rome must have seemed more and more foreign to them. Whatever the cause, the religious Reformation swept through Europe in the 1500s and provided a religious basis for the political rivalries that were already causing problems.

While the recent discovery of printing had allowed greater communication among the European nations, that was balanced by the fact that, for the first time, firearms were widely available. Warfare had become very deadly indeed, and small, well-armed groups could have great power. Spain, France, and England were the strongest superpowers of that time. Of these, England and Spain were the great sea powers. Control of the sea, or at least great strength at sea, is needed to become a colonial power. When the colonies are three thousand miles away across a great ocean, people and goods must travel by sea. If those people do not have a navy strong enough to protect them on their voyage, they will stay at home. If the colonies are not protected from invasion by sea, then they will be lost rather quickly.

The New World was settled by people from many different nations. But only those with strong navies, Spain and England, kept large colonial empires for a long period of time. The other nations, such as Holland, Sweden, and even France, lost their colonies very quickly. In the 1500s, Spain had a colonial empire that involved most of South America and Central America and some of the west coast of the modern United States. England made no permanent settlements until the early 1600s, but it was interested in the Caribbean Islands from the very beginning. The gold was not there, but the key to the gold was.

Even in remote Puerto Rico, the problems of Europe could not be escaped. Early in 1522, there was a report that the French had sent three ships with seven hundred men to capture the island. In response, the Spanish authorities built a wooden wall at the entrance to San Juan Harbor. The Spanish were lucky that the French ships never arrived because this simple battlement would not have lasted very long. By 1530, a stone building, *Casa Blanca*, or the White House, had been set up to provide a place of shelter during an attack. Even this strengthening of the defenses was not very significant.

The Spanish on Puerto Rico were aware of how easily they could be defeated by an armed enemy, and they kept urging Spain to provide more help to them. By 1532, construction of *La Fortaleza*, a fortress at the edge of the shoreline, had begun. This was completed in 1540 and was followed immediately by the construction of *El Morro*, a major fort at the entrance to the harbor. Both *La Fortaleza* and *El Morro* still stand today, symbols of the skill of the builders of the earlier culture of Puerto Rico.

San Juan was the jewel of Puerto Rico. It was the home

of most of the island's inhabitants and, because of its great harbor, the military and commercial center as well. But Puerto Rico was still an island, surrounded by water and able to be invaded at any point, not just at San Juan. Villa de San German was the other major settlement at that time, and it was located on Puerto Rico's west coast with no real defenses at all. It was subjected to regular raids from French ships, and its center was moved many times to locations that provided greater protection from the sea raiders.

The Spanish colonial rulers saw their colonies as profit-making centers. They had no plans to spend money on them; they just wanted to get money out of them. In order to make the most possible money out of Puerto Rico, Spain would not allow other nations to trade with its colony or allow its colonists to trade with other nations. That may seem unfair. But to the Spanish government, it was not unfair at all. Spain had paid for the ships that discovered Puerto Rico and it had shipped the colonists and the soldiers that protected them to Puerto Rico at its own expense. Spain owned the island and, in a sense, it owned the colonists as well. It was only fair, then, that Spain receive the profit from this venture.

But there were two problems with the Spanish thinking. First, if Spain was to become rich from Puerto Rico and its other colonies, what about the colonists? It was they who abandoned their homes in Spain, took a dangerous voyage across the Atlantic, settled in a new and foreign place, cleared the fields, looked for the gold, and ran the risk of being attacked and killed by soldiers from other nations. Didn't they deserve a chance to become rich from their efforts? By limiting them to trading only with Spain, Spain forced them to deal with only one buyer. There was no guarantee that this buyer would come up with the best price, or even a fair price, for their goods. They saw no reason to work very hard when the profit went to Spain.

The other problem was that Spain was thousands of difficult sea miles away from Puerto Rico. Communication was very slow, and real supervision was even slower. The king of Spain could give all of the orders that he wanted, but he had no way of enforcing them on the spot. So despite the rule requiring Puerto Rico to trade only with Spain, the colonists were really free to do whatever they wanted to do. They just had to avoid bragging about it. As a result, there was a great deal of illegal trade.

The Spanish Caribbean colonies gained some wealth from this trade, though not the great riches that many of the colonists had hoped for. Nonetheless, they were able to build towns that would have been recognized as substantial in rural Spain. A typical Spanish colonial town might have fifty or more houses in it and one or two public buildings. The public buildings were centers of government and trade and they also served as community centers where the people of the town might gather for entertainment.

The private homes had a broad range of architecture and of furnishings. A wealthy home was typically made of brick or adobe and had several rooms as well as a walled courtyard. The walls were very thick to provide a natural insulation. Glass for some windows was imported from Italy, and the furnishings very likely came from Spain. Slaves lived in a separate part of the house and were responsible for cleaning and cooking. The food was somewhat different from the food of Spain. While some European meats such as beef and pork were eaten, local seafood and vegetables and grains had become a major part of the diet of the people.

The poorer Spanish residents had much smaller houses made from the same materials. Their furnishings and clothing were all locally made, since they could not afford to ship in expensive goods from Europe. Instead of fine china, they used cruder local pottery, and there was no glass in their windows.

The public buildings usually included a church. Indeed, this was often the largest building in the town. The Spanish were almost all Catholics, and they saw the spread of Christianity as one of their main purposes in coming to the New World. Priests were always included in the colonizing groups. They provided a core of educated people who could teach and lead the new colonists. They taught Latin free to anyone who was interested in learning and, by the early 1600s, had established a system of what we would now call grammar schools. The Indians and Africans received some education as well, since the ability to read the Bible was considered to be an important part of religious instruction for them.

But school was not a regular part of life for very many people. Even the small number of educated people had gone to school for only a short period, to learn to read and write. Agriculture and trade were the lifeblood of the colony, and one did not have to be very well educated to participate in either of those activities.

The church was also responsible for the medical needs of the people, and hospitals were established in the two major cities, San Juan and San German, in the 1500s.

Illegal trade brought the colonists into regular contact with ships from other European nations. They traded sugar and coffee for cloth and other manufactured goods and for slaves. In Puerto Rico, as in the American colonies, slavery had made profit from large farms possible. This trade contact with foreigners made other Europeans aware of Puerto Rico's importance. And still its defenses were too weak to protect against any serious attack.

The situation became dangerous for Puerto Rico after 1588. In that year, the great Spanish Armada was destroyed by a combination of the skill of the English fleet under Sir Francis Drake and a great storm in the Atlantic. This single event nearly destroyed Spain's sea power while English strength at sea increased greatly. Spain had taken its American colonies because of its strength at sea. Without that strength, it could well lose them.

The alternative to defending colonies with naval power was to strengthen the defenses of the colonies themselves. With the defeat of the armada, a new wave of building for defense took place in Puerto Rico. At the time of the armada, Puerto Rico was defended by only fifty soldiers and some volunteer colonists. This handful of defenders was poorly equipped, and the soldiers' pay often did not arrive.

To improve the situation, the governor of the island, then Diego Menendez de Valdes, was given the additional title of captain-general. Under his leadership and under plans devised by the military engineer, Bautista Antonelli, the defenses of San Juan were greatly improved. A new fort was built at *El Morro,* and other existing fortifications were strengthened. One hundred fifty soldiers were added to the island's defenses, and their pay was to come directly from the *situado,* a fund from the treasury of New Spain (Mexico). This money was sent by ship whenever the governor of New Spain felt that he could afford to send it. This meant that it sometimes did not arrive for years, and in the meantime, the governor of Puerto Rico had to borrow from the handful of wealthy residents to pay for the island's defenses.

The English, who had already landed troops on Puerto Rico, supposedly to get food but probably to spy on the military situation, grew bolder after the defeat of the armada. Sir Francis Drake, the hero of the armada, proposed to Queen Elizabeth I a plan for the capture of Spain's island colonies. At first, the queen had some doubts about Drake's plan, but word that a vast fortune in gold and silver had been brought to Puerto Rico for shipment to Spain made her approve the proposal.

In 1595, Drake sailed for the Caribbean with twenty-seven ships and four thousand five hundred troops. He ran into trouble almost from the start. An attempt to capture the Canary Islands, off the coast of Africa, failed. Then one of his biggest ships was attacked and destroyed by a Spanish fleet. When he finally arrived in Puerto

Rico, he found its defenses in better shape than he had imagined.

The same Spanish fleet that had sunk Drake's ship had hurried to San Juan to advise the captain-general of the danger. Over fifteen hundred sailors joined the island's garrison of three hundred, which brought the number of troops to eighteen hundred. Two of the Spanish ships were sunk at the entrance to the harbor to block Drake's fleet from entering. Seventy artillery pieces lined the harbor as well. The English fleet arrived off San Juan Harbor on November 22, 1595. It came under fire immediately, and Drake withdrew from cannon range. At night, he sent fifteen hundred men in small boats to board the Spanish ships and burn them. The attack failed, and the English lost nearly four hundred men.

Drake wisely withdrew and circled the island, looking for another means of attack. But the treasure was in San Juan, and San Juan was too well defended. It would give Drake no glory to attack one of the small coastal villages with his great fleet and come home with a pocketful of treasure. In early December, he sailed home for England.

But there was no great joy in Puerto Rico over Drake's defeat. The people knew that Drake and the English were interested in their island. It might have taken more ships and more men to capture it, but the English had plenty of both. The next year saw even more work on the defenses and a doubling of the garrison of professional soldiers, which now numbered more than four hundred.

The Puerto Ricans were ready for their English enemy, but they were not ready for an even deadlier one—disease. An epidemic of smallpox struck the soldiers in 1597, and many of them died. The epidemic also slowed the work on the fortifications. In June of 1598, another English fleet arrived, and the situation was dangerous. On June 16, the Earl of Cumberland, the commander of the fleet, landed a thousand men slightly up the coast from San Juan, away from the defenses of the city.

The English troops defended by the great guns of the British fleet offshore moved by land toward San Juan. The city at that time was centered on an island separated from the mainland of Puerto Rico by a narrow body of water. The two were connected by Soldier's Bridge. The defenders of the city had burned the bridge and guarded the shore area leading to the island. Although there were few of them, the fortress there, *Boqueron*, was a strong one and had six cannons. The English, unable to capture the site, retreated.

The next morning, Cumberland launched a second attack, sending two groups of soldiers at the *Boqueron* from opposite sides. The fort fell, and the English moved on to San Juan. The four hundred defenders of the city had moved into *El Morro*. The fortress was strong enough to withstand an attack, but the defenders were not strong enough to resist a siege. They needed food and water, and there was no one to break through the English troops to supply them. After fifteen days of siege, starvation had become a reality, and the governor surrendered to the English. The Spanish defenders were sent to Jamaica, and the English flag flew over Puerto Rico.

Cumberland's rule over the island was short-lived,

though. His men fell by the hundreds to the same small-pox epidemic that had so weakened the island's defenses. Moreover, the Puerto Ricans were not happy about the conquest and did everything in their power to make life unpleasant for the new English rulers. On August 27, after only seven weeks, Cumberland withdrew from Puerto Rico, but only after burning most of the houses in the city, destroying crops, and taking loot, including two thousand slaves and all the church bells on the island. Some English remained for a week or two longer, but Puerto Rico was fully under Spanish rule again by early September.

Five years later, after Queen Elizabeth's death, King James I of England agreed to a peace treaty with Spain. The English abandoned the idea of South American colonies and, instead, four years later, started their first New World colony in Jamestown, Virginia.

But Puerto Rico was still not safe from outside attack. So work continued on the island's defenses, still slowed by disease and a lack of troops.

The next enemy was the Dutch. For a small nation, Holland had a fairly large navy. It had colonies around the world, and the Dutch East and West India companies were among the world's great trading enterprises. The Dutch had some colonies in the Caribbean area and were interested in expanding them.

In 1625, a general working for the Dutch West India Company in the Caribbean, named Boudewijn Hendrikszoon, led a fleet of seventeen ships to Puerto Rico. The captain-general of San Juan, Juan de Haro, expected that the Dutch, like the English before them, would try to make a landing outside of San Juan and then move by land to attack the forts. Instead, the Dutch surprised the defenders by sailing straight into the harbor and landing their troops.

Once again, the Puerto Rican "army," this time numbering only three hundred and thirty people, moved into *El Morro*. Once again, the invaders laid siege to the fortress. But this time their siege failed. While the Dutch burned part of the city, de Haro organized a group of one hundred fifty soldiers to stage a raid on the attackers. At the same time, a group of soldiers from other parts of the island arrived and attacked the Dutch from a different direction. Confused and with a large number of dead and wounded, the Dutch retreated to their ships and sailed away after a month of siege.

The need for better defenses was now clear to everyone. The colonists of Puerto Rico were brave, and luck had been on their side, but such things were no substitute for a sound plan for defending the colony. Several plans were considered involving additional forts and harbor defenses. The plan that was finally adopted involved building a wall around the entire city, making it one large fortress with no weak spots. Much of the labor force of the colony was put to work.

By 1638, the enormous task was half-completed. The walls, parts of which can still be seen today, were over twenty-two feet high and more than eighteen feet thick. They would be difficult to climb over and impossible for all but the most powerful cannons to breach. After this initial burst of energy, things slowed down quite a bit, and it took more than a century to complete the task.

But even though the city now had great walls, it still lacked a sufficient number of soldiers to defend them. The garrison remained at four hundred. To make up for this weakness, armed citizens groups, militia, were organized in every major population center. Although they were trained and organized, they were not very well armed. Their weapons, as often as not, were sticks, or long knives called *machetes*, used for chopping down plants. These weapons were not enough to provide for a proper defense, but we shall hear more of the *machete* later on.

In the seventeenth and eighteenth centuries, Puerto Rico slowly evolved from a settlement, where people stayed for a short time and then returned home, into a colony. Finally, it became something harder to describe. It became a place that was under the rule of an overseas sovereign who had little political authority in the island itself. New generations born on the island had no particular allegiance to the king of Spain. They were Puerto Ricans and they had an outlook on life that was different from that of their Spanish rulers. They inherited a Spanish culture and adopted a Caribbean culture. They were people of two worlds and of neither world. This sense of being different from the people who had political control over them would last until the present day.

In these years, the people of the island changed. A small population shrank, then grew very rapidly. Gradually, they forged a link with the English colonies in North

America. Thus, the place that we now know as Puerto Rico came into being. The Indian population died out. The slave population, brought in from Africa to replace the Indians, grew larger, and an economy at long last independent of Spain prospered.

# 4

# A New Society

*The Spanish viewed Puerto Rico primarily as a fortress, a* defense post in the Caribbean designed to protect the rich colonies on the mainland of South America. Certainly they did not see it as much more than that, as a brief look at the political and economic history of the colony will make clear.

In 1509, King Ferdinand of Spain appointed Juan Ponce de León as the first governor of Puerto Rico. But in 1511, the Spanish courts ruled that the king did not have that right. Instead, they said, Christopher Columbus's family had the right to name officials in Puerto Rico. Columbus had died in 1505, and his rights in the New World were the only property he had left his family. This meant that Puerto Rico was a proprietary colony, one owned by private parties. Odd as that may seem to us today, it was not at all unusual. Several American states began their history as proprietary colonies.

In 1536, the Columbus family sold their rights back to the king. This incident shows that the Spanish viewed Puerto Rico as a piece of property, not as a place where citizens of Spain with political rights lived and worked. Again, this was not an unusual attitude. What was unusual is that the attitude would last for centuries, long after other European powers had recognized some degree of political rights in their colonies in the New World.

It is important to understand both sides of this matter. To Spain, Puerto Rico *was* a fortress and little more. It was a place where a handful of their soldiers stayed for brief periods to provide some defense for a harbor that was a useful stopover for Spanish galleons bringing the riches of Peru and Mexico back to Spain. The permanent colonists were not very important. They provided necessary harbor services and they produced a small amount of the products that were wanted in Spain, but not enough to make the colony an independent economic unit.

The colonists must have had several different views, depending upon their role in society. The soldiers and political officials who came and went probably saw Puerto Rico in much the same way as the Spanish government did. They were there on official business and returned, after a while, to their real lives in Spain or to other positions in other colonies. New colonists were probably torn. They had been born and raised in Spain, but in coming to Puerto Rico they may have committed themselves to living there for the rest of their lives. So they probably felt both Spanish and Puerto Rican. Their children born in Puerto Rico with no knowledge of the Spanish homeland probably felt more Puerto Rican than Spanish. As one generation succeeded another, the identity with Spain lessened.

The first generation must have longed for Spanish food

and familiar weather and geographic features. The second generation would have known some Spanish food because some would have been shipped in from Spain, but it would have known little of Spanish weather or mountains. Each generation after that would have had fewer and fewer links with Spain. The wealthy residents would have gone back for visits or sent their children to school in Spain, but most people were like George Washington in America, a man who never saw his grandparents' homeland.

So two groups emerged in Puerto Rico. The first was a wealthy ruling class with strong links to Spain. These ties were political, economic, and social. Bankers and traders depended for their livelihood on good relations with Spain. Political officials depended for their power on the support of the Spanish king. In matters of dress, education, literature, and friends, they also looked to Spain. These people would have frequent reasons to visit Spain and to socialize with Spanish people who came to visit from Spain. Their customs, clothing, and furniture were more likely to be Spanish, compared with that of other residents of Puerto Rico.

The second group was the poorer people whose links with Spain were not long lasting. If they had been born there, they never returned. If they had been born poor in Puerto Rico, the business of life in Puerto Rico was probably much more important to them than their parents' memories of being poor in Spain.

The real settlement of Puerto Rico began in 1508, but a generation later, in 1531, the Spanish population was only 426 people, most of whom were soldiers. Even this tiny number would decrease over the next few years. The conquest of Peru and of Mexico provided the promise of gold and silver, which was what had brought many of these people to the New World. They had been disappointed to find no great wealth in Puerto Rico, and the chance to make up for this loss proved irresistible.

This bothered the colonial government a great deal. Soldiers were deserting to hunt for wealth. Puerto Rico's role as a fortress required that there be farms to feed the troops and troops to feed. In order to keep the population and to attract new settlers, the government arranged for loans to build sugar mills. These provided a source of income for the settlers, but could not protect them from the diseases that had so devastated the island's defenses.

Just as the Indians had no natural resistance to the diseases that the Europeans brought with them, so the Europeans had no natural resistance to the diseases that they found in Puerto Rico. Sickness and tropical hurricanes combined with the lack of a chance to become wealthy to keep the population low well into the 1700s. The population of San Juan was 170 in 1581; 500 in 1647; and, by 1673, it had reached only 820. Even that small population was reduced in 1690 when a wave of epidemics killed hundreds of settlers.

The slave population was larger. In 1531 when the Spanish population on the whole island of Puerto Rico was 426, the African population was 2,264. Sugar was a plantation crop, and it was the main crop of Puerto Rico. There were no machines to harvest sugar. It was harvested by hand, and the hands were the hands of slaves.

Slavery was a major issue in Puerto Rico just as it was in the American states. From the very beginning, there were people who detested the idea of holding another human being in slavery. On the other hand, there were many people who did not believe, or chose not to believe, that the Africans were human beings in the same way that they were. These people had a strong economic motivation to enforce their beliefs. Without slaves, there would be no sugar crop. Spanish farmers had not moved to Puerto Rico to work in the fields under the hot sun. They could do that at home with crops that were familiar to them. Spanish farmers moved to Puerto Rico because they wanted to become landowners. They would manage the land and let the slaves do the hard work of actually farming it. There were few Indians left to help with the crop, and even these were just slaves of a different color.

The settlers were given land by the crown. Between two hundred and fourteen hundred acres were granted to each settler who would agree to build a house, farm the land, and stay for up to five years. There were two basic types of farming: subsistence farming, in which the farmer raised food crops for the use of his own family and some small sales in local markets; and export farming, in which the farmer raised crops such as sugar, coffee, or spices, which were in great demand in Europe.

Sugar and the other export crops required a great deal of land and some processing. Shipping sugarcane to Europe would waste too much space in the ships. Instead, the cane was processed in Puerto Rico and the sugar shipped back to Europe for sale. Export farming also required ships, so the export farmers needed a great deal of money for land, slaves to harvest the crop, mills to process the sugarcane, and ships to transport the sugar to market. A shortage of any one of these items meant that the farmer did not make money.

By 1582, there were eleven sugar mills operating in Puerto Rico. But ships were in short supply, so twenty years later the number of mills that the island could support had dropped to eight. By the seventeenth century, tobacco and ginger had become the most important crops.

Even with improvements in farming and with an increase in illegal trade with other nations, Puerto Rico was poor. Local taxes were not enough to pay for governing and defending the island. The royal payments were still needed.

Just as the island was not economically independent, so too its political life was tied to Spain's. The island's governor represented the king and had final authority in ruling Puerto Rico. Beneath him was the *Cabildo,* a kind of city council. There were two of these in the early days of Puerto Rico. One was based in San Juan and governed the eastern half of the island, known as the *Partido de San Juan.* The other was based in San German and governed the western half of Puerto Rico, the *Partido de la Villa.*

The *Cabildo* was not a democratic institution. Its members consisted of two *Alcaldes,* or judges, who were elected by the other members of the *Cabildo,* the *Regidores.* The *Regidores* in turn were selected by the governor, though the post was sometimes sold to the highest bidder. These officials selected the rest of the public officers in their area. One result of this procedure was that these other officers were often friends or relatives of the *Cabildo* members. Thus, the group of people who really ran Puerto Rico were from a small number of wealthy families. The same thing could be said of almost every European colony in the New World.

The *Cabildo* itself reported to the *Audiencia,* the Spanish governing body in the Caribbean, and the *Audiencia* was supervised by the Council of the Indies in Spain itself. Puerto Rico, like the rest of the Spanish colonies, was not self-governing.

The power of the *Cabildo* was largely commercial. It had the authority to set quotas for farmers and the power to distribute vacant land. These powers were often used to give even greater wealth to the family and friends of the members. It also served as a court on land matters. The *Cabildo* was responsible for roads, bridges, cemeteries, wells, and other public works. It sponsored festivals and was responsible for public health.

The *Cabildo,* in short, was the center of public life. Its decisions affected everyone on the island. But the island was still a lonely and thinly populated place. Only a few of its inhabitants were wealthy, and there was no great likelihood that many more would be. As the 1600s came to a close, Puerto Rico was not much different than it had been in the 1500s. The English colonies to the north were growing larger and stronger. The Spanish colonies to the west had attracted many settlers with the lure of gold, and they were developing a form of independence from Spain that would not come to Puerto Rico until the very end of its days as a Spanish colony.

The 1700s saw a maturing in most of the Caribbean colonies. The French, the English, and the Danes all had major colonies in the islands, and these had developed strong farming economies. The European demand for sugar and spices was growing, and larger and larger fleets were used to meet that demand. Attacks by one country on another country's shipping were common. As often as not, these attacks were not carried out by the official navy, but by privateers. Privateers were sailors licensed by one country to act as a kind of unofficial navy. In theory, their license was to provide defense. In fact, they were often just licensed pirates.

Privateers became wealthy through plundering merchant ships of other nations. Because the ships they commanded were armed, they also had a certain military power. It is not surprising, then, that some privateers came to be politically powerful figures in Puerto Rico. One Puerto Rican privateer, Miguel Henriquez, was even knighted by the king of Spain.

Other nations, of course, were not very happy with the privateers. The English considered themselves the masters of the sea. They had the most to gain from open commerce on the waters, since they had the largest fleet of the times. The actions of Spanish privateers angered the English and gave them another excuse to try to take control of the Spanish islands for themselves.

The privateering and other conflicts between Spain and England led, in 1739, to the War of Jenkins' Ear.

This war certainly has one of history's most interesting names. It received that title because it began after an English sea captain, Robert Jenkins, claimed that Spanish officials in the Caribbean had had his ear cut off. While Captain Jenkins was probably very unhappy about the incident, the real cause of the war was more likely the desire of the English to gain control of Spain's colonies in the New World. They certainly tried to do so. Two fleets launched attacks. One, under Admiral Vernon, threatened Puerto Rico and briefly took control of Panama.

The Spanish authorities had been slow to recognize that for Puerto Rico to be a successful fortress, it had to be more than a fortress. If its only real purpose was military, then it would be up to Spain to hire and support troops for the island's defense. If, instead, it was a full-fledged and self-supporting colony, then the colonists would have a stake in protecting it. There would be a large enough population so that soldiers could be found and trained on the island itself and the island economy would generate enough money to help support those soldiers and to build and maintain the fortifications that were necessary.

By the mid-1700s, the king realized that something had to be done about Puerto Rico. Smuggling was a major industry there, so that Spain was not gaining as much from the island's limited trade as it might have. The activities of the privateers were a source of continuing friction with other nations, and the interest of the English in taking control of the island had not faded.

In 1765, the king sent to Puerto Rico Marshal Alejandro O'Reilly. He was a man of great energy and skill. He examined virtually every aspect of Puerto Rican life and provided the king not only with a report on the present state of affairs in Puerto Rico, but also with a comprehensive plan for improving the situation on the island.

O'Reilly's report is one of the most important documents of the Spanish colonial period. It shows us a society that had changed a great deal since the 1600s. The population had increased to nearly forty-five thousand people, of which only five thousand were slaves. Three-fourths of the people were under forty.

O'Reilly learned that, despite the Spanish monopoly on trade with Puerto Rico, there was virtually no trade between the colony and the motherland. This was a sure sign that smuggling was widespread. The colonists must be trading with someone, since they produced very little of what they needed themselves. If they were not trading with Spain, then they must be trading illegally.

Even if they were not trading with Spain, they were certainly being supported by Spain. Ninety percent of the government costs for the island were made by payments from the Spanish treasury. Only 10 percent came from taxes paid by the islanders themselves.

Though the island was poor and the islanders were not doing much to help their own situation, there were reasons for this and there were grounds to believe that the situation could be changed for the better. Soldiers were still a large portion of Puerto Rico's population. Soldiers produce nothing and they consume quite a bit. If a greater part of the population had been employed in farming or industry, the amount produced obviously would have been greater. And the resources for much greater production were available. Only 5 percent of the land had been cleared for farming at that time. If more land had been cleared, there would have been more farmland available for more colonists. Here O'Reilly supported a new system of distribution of land. Rather than having the land distributed by the *Cabildo,* he urged that the king take over all unused land to distribute to new settlers who were willing and able to farm it.

At the same time, the strict trade laws needed to be changed. As it was, Puerto Rico could trade legally only with Spain. Even with Spain, trade was limited to just a few ports, and goods could legally be shipped only from San Juan. These laws were being widely ignored, but at the same time they were hampering the growth of legal commerce. People used up energy and resources in smuggling that could be used, instead, for legal trade with Spain, if the products of Puerto Rico could be traded to the highest bidder there, instead of to a monopoly of merchants in Seville through a monopoly of shippers in San Juan.

O'Reilly supported changes in the trade law that would recognize the widespread illegal trade and allow the crown as well as the settlers to benefit from it.

O'Reilly was a soldier by profession, so he did not ignore the military needs of Puerto Rico. He found that the officers were corrupt and that there was very little discipline among the soldiers in the garrison. He fined the officers who had ignored their duties and reorganized the citizen militia for protection of the coastal villages beyond the San Juan area.

O'Reilly's report marks the first time that the government in Spain had paid much serious attention to the needs of Puerto Rico. The *situado* (the payment to Puerto Rico from the Spanish riches in Mexico) was greatly increased. The work on the walls around San Juan was begun again. A new governor, Don Miguel de Muesas, was appointed, and he made significant changes in the political structure of Puerto Rico. He founded seven new towns, gathering people who had been scattered in small villages into larger and more defensible cities. He started and supported new schools. These schools were open to everyone without regard to race or wealth.

By the 1770s, Puerto Rico was not yet a thriving colony, but it was a place with a future. The houses were fancier and sturdier than they had been in the early settlement days. Thick stone walls kept the houses cool. Large openings in the walls could be closed with shutters to keep out the rain or opened to let in a breeze. The churches and government buildings were larger and more impressive. These ancient church buildings, many of which still stand in Puerto Rico today, are classic examples of Spanish-American architecture. A cultural life was developing. Jose Campeche was the first great Puerto Rican painter, and he lived and worked at this time. Roads and bridges were being built throughout the island. It was the beginning of a new era in the life of Puerto Rico. Change was everywhere in the air.

But a change of a different sort was starting to be felt in other parts of the New World. In the English colonies of America and on the nearby French island of Haiti, revolution was coming. The revolutions represented a new spirit in colonial life, a spirit of independence, and an identity unlike that of the homeland. Soon that same spirit would come to the Spanish colonies and would have a major effect on the island of Puerto Rico. While Puerto Rico itself did not join in this revolutionary movement, it was far more than just a spectator to the events, and the results of these revolutions would be felt for decades to come.

*A photograph from 1903 shows the monument to Christopher Columbus erected to mark the four hundredth anniversary of his arrival in Puerto Rico in 1493.*

*A seventeenth-century view of San Juan shows more a fortress than a city.*

PORTO RICO

*This photograph, taken before the turn of the century shows the great thickness of the walls built to protect San Juan and the diversity of the Puerto Rican people.*

WELL, I HARDLY KNOW WHICH TO TAKE FIRST!

*The creator of this cartoon was one of many Americans who thought the Spanish-American War was just an excuse to seize territory.*

*The naval bombardment of San Juan by American ships in May of 1898* "y

*A road built by the early Spanish conquerors cuts through the coffee-growing mountainous region of central Puerto Rico.*

*The house of a well-to-do family in Puerto Rico at the turn of the century.*

*Opposite page: A* jíbaro *works in the sugar fields wearing the traditional straw hat and cuts cane with a machete.*

*Theodore Roosevelt in his Rough Rider uniform in Puerto Rico in 1898. His son would become one of the better colonial governors, and his cousin Franklin would seek a New Deal in Puerto Rico as well as the United States.*

# 5
# The Age of Revolution

*A colonial empire has its own life span.* It can exist only so long as the colonists desire to remain linked with the mother country or the mother country is strong enough to force the colony to remain linked, whether the colonists want that or not.

The colonists' desires are affected by a number of issues, such as the strength of the emotional and financial links with the mother country and the sense the colonists have of whether they are being treated fairly or not.

The mother country's ability to use force to keep the colony depends upon how close the two are physically, what other military obligations the mother country has, and the military strength of the colony.

The links between mother country and colony are affected greatly by the passage of time. When a colony is new, the affections for the mother country and the dependency on the mother country remain very high. At the same time, the military and economic strength of the colony is low. As time passes, the links to the mother country grow weaker, and the ability to survive independently of the mother country grows stronger.

Toward the end of the eighteenth century, the links between the New World colonies and their European mother countries had grown weak. Generations had been born and raised in the New World. At the same time, the colonies had grown in population and military strength. Such a situation was certain to lead to an effort to separate from the mother countries. The only question was where it would happen first. Actually, that was not much of a question either. The English colonies in North America were the most likely spot by far. Their ties to the mother country were very weak for a number of reasons. Many of the colonists were not English. They had come from Sweden, Holland, France, and other countries as well as from England. Even among those who did come from England, there was little connection with that island. Many had fled England for religious or political reasons.

In addition, these colonies had grown quite large and powerful, both militarily and economically. Finally, the colonists were very upset with the way they were being treated by England. They felt that they were being used economically and that their liberties were being unfairly interfered with.

While England was the most powerful nation on earth at that time, still the colonists were in a fairly strong position to resist. England was faraway, and English troops obviously had to travel by sea. There were local militia everywhere in the colonies and strong leadership trained, like George Washington, in the battles of the

French and Indian Wars. Finally, there were many nations with an interest in supporting the colonists in a drive for independence. France and Spain would be able to increase trade with the American colonies if they were independent. Independence would also weaken England's international position, and that too was valuable to the other European powers. These nations would also be aided if England was tied up in a conflict with its own colonies. In such a case, it would have less energy left to interfere with other nations and their colonies.

For these reasons, the American Revolution should have come as no surprise when it began in 1775. It should also have come as no surprise to the other European powers that they would be next on the list. The French and Spanish colonies of the New World watched the American Revolution with interest, and it did not take them very long to catch up.

Haiti was the first to follow the American example. Here too the revolt seems inevitable. Haiti, then the French colony of Saint Dominique, was a warehouse for slaves. By 1785, there were more than five hundred thousand slaves, most of them African. They were ruled by a very small number of French plantation owners. The slaves obviously had very little love for the French homeland and very strong feelings that they were being exploited politically and economically. In addition, the outbreak of revolution in France itself, in 1789, opened the door wide to rebellion. France was much too occupied with the battle going on at home to send troops to a small island colony in a faraway place.

In 1791, the Haitian slaves revolted, and though their struggle took many years and many lives, they became the founders of the second free nation in the New World. The Haitian revolt inspired other slave revolts, which were not successful. However, the Spanish colonies were spared such revolts because in many ways the Spanish took care of their slaves much better than the English or the French did. They were not treated as harshly in their work and in their lives, and for them too the opportunities for freedom from slavery were much greater. It must be remembered, though, that they were still slaves, and living in slavery is degrading, even if one is physically comfortable.

The Spanish colonies were also prosperous. Mexico City was the third-largest city in the world. The four provinces of the Spanish colonies—Peru, New Spain, La Plata, and New Granada—all had developed agriculture and mining.

The Spanish colonies were different in other ways also. The colonists were divided between *peninsulares,* those born in Spain, and *creoles,* those born in the New World. The *peninsulares,* were the ruling class, large in numbers and even larger in power. While there were some local militia in the Spanish colonies, the Spanish armies were larger and more experienced. The *creoles* had neither the military strength nor the military leadership to take on the *peninsulares.* The *creole* ties to the homeland were also stronger than in the English colonies. They were united not just by language and culture, but by strong religious beliefs as well. While the English colonists represented many different religions, the Spanish colonists were overwhelmingly Roman Catholic, and the church was supported by the Spanish monarchy.

The Spanish colonies had also come under attack from the French and the English, and Spanish colonists feared being conquered by one of those nations. Unity with Spain provided a kind of protection against other nations.

At the end of the 1700s, then, the Spanish colonies did not seem to be likely places for revolution. All of this was suddenly to change, not because of revolution in the New World but because of revolution in the Old World. The leader of the revolution in the Spanish colonies was not a Spaniard and would never set foot in the New World. The leader was Napoleon Bonaparte.

When Napoleon became emperor of France, he set off more than a decade of war in Europe. That war used up most of Europe's military strength and caused the European nations, especially Spain, to ignore their New World colonies.

In 1810, Napoleon took control of Spain and placed his brother Joseph on the Spanish throne. Napoleon's military adventures caused the Spanish to focus their military strength in Europe. It also broke down the political power in the New World of the *peninsulares*. They no longer had the military strength to defend the colonies that they ruled. The seasoned Spanish troops who had formed the bulk of the defenses had returned to fight in Europe. The *peninsulares* had to rely on *creole* militia to fight off foreign attacks. The militia units were expanded, and there were many *creole* officers who became the leaders of the colonial defense forces.

Napoleon also encouraged the independence of the

colonies. He granted them much more freedom than the Spanish kings had done, and he even stated that it was fair and just that they should be free from Spanish control.

Napoleon's rule over Spain did not last long. When King Ferdinand VII came back to the throne in 1814, he attempted to turn back the clock to the pre-Napoleonic days. But that was impossible. The power of the *peninsulares* had faded, and there was too much for the king of Spain to do in Europe to allow him to spend much time or energy restoring the lost power in the colonies.

One colony after another sought independence. They were aided by leaders such as Simon Bolivar, a Venezuelan, and Jose San Martin, a veteran of the Spanish wars against Napoleon, who traveled from colony to colony leading and supporting the revolutionaries. Spain did regain some of its power as years went by, but not enough to mount an effort to take back the colonies. In addition, the United States had, in 1823, issued the Monroe Doctrine, which announced that the United States would regard an attack on any free nation in the New World as an attack upon the United States itself. The United States was probably not strong enough to make good on that threat, but England supported the Monroe Doctrine as well, since it was interested in free trade with the new nations.

By the end of the 1820s, there were ten independent nations in Spanish America. There would be further political changes in those areas, but the basic issue—independence—was settled.

These fifty years of revolution, from the start of the

American Revolution until the end of the Spanish colonial revolutions, had surprisingly little effect on Puerto Rico. Indeed, if anything, the revolutions in South and Central America actually strengthened the Spanish hold on the island.

The first effect of the revolutionary period on Puerto Rico was that the *situado* was no longer being sent from Mexico. While this fund had never been a reliable source of income for the island, it disappeared entirely when rebellion struck in Mexico.

The second effect was more positive. During the period when Napoleon was battling for control of Spain, the Spanish people most active in opposing him were also those who favored more freedom than the king had allowed. They established a government (the *Junta*, or committee) separate from that of Napoleon's brother Joseph. While this *Junta* was almost powerless in Spain, it was the only government the colonies had. Napoleon had sent an envoy to Puerto Rico to take over the government there, but the envoy spent his time in a jail cell in *El Morro*. In 1809, the *Junta* issued a decree concerning the colonies. The decree stated that the colonists were politically equal to other Spaniards and should have representation in the government.

The representative who was chosen by Puerto Rico was Ramon Power y Giralt, a thirty-four-year-old naval officer. Power was well educated and had visited many countries. He went to Spain with orders from his fellow colonists.

The first order was that if Spain fell entirely to Napoleon the islanders should be free to govern their own lives. He was also directed to seek support for a greatly expanded educational system. At that time, Puerto Rico had only a handful of elementary schools and two high schools for a population of over two hundred thousand.

He was to ask for other public works as well, including hospitals, roads, and bridges. The colonists also wanted to elect local officials, remove restrictions on farming and trade, distribute the available land among the people, decrease taxes, and encourage foreign trade.

This list of needs was very similar to what O'Reilly had proposed to the king fifty years before. Power went to Spain to become the first Puerto Rican member of the *Cortes*, or parliament. He was unanimously elected as the first vice president of that body and he had some success in winning the reforms he had been sent to achieve. The *Cortes* approved legislation creating the office of intendancy. The intendant was to be the civilian leader separate from the military office of captain-general. The *Cortes* also approved the opening of more ports and the elimination of some taxes and customs duties. Greater power was given to local government on the island, including authority over tax collection and the distribution of land. These provisions and others were contained in the *Ley Power*, or Power Act.

More important, perhaps, than the Power Act was the Constitution of 1812. This was adopted by the *Cortes* and included provisions guaranteeing Puerto Ricans and other Spanish colonists a set of rights, such as free speech, very similar to those found in the American Bill of Rights.

Though the Constitution of 1812 lasted only until King Ferdinand regained the throne in 1814, it was to be revived later on, and its concepts probably came closest to capturing the desires of the Puerto Rican people in the 1800s. It became important as a symbol of what could be.

The institution of the intendancy remained after Ferdinand took back the throne. Alejandro Ramirez was chosen by Spain to be the first intendant. He was a man of great experience in colonial government, and he moved quickly when he arrived in Puerto Rico.

He set up a system of direct taxation. Previously, tax collectors had been hired who would themselves pay all the taxes owed and then collect from the people who owed them. This system was corrupt, for the tax collectors had a tendency to underestimate the tax owed when they paid it and to overestimate the tax owed when they collected it. In the new tax system, the tax was based on an estimate of how much wealth a community had. The community would then pay a tax based on that estimate. The amount of money collected under the new tax system was nearly double that collected under the old system.

Ramirez also began to circulate paper money instead of the metal coins that had been the only currency before. He established newspapers and encouraged developments in agriculture, especially the use of modern methods of farming.

With the return of the king, a struggle could well have taken place like the revolutions on the South American continent. The Puerto Ricans had tasted independence, and they liked it. The king was aware of the fact that his empire was falling apart around him, and he took some steps to hold on to the parts that were left. In Puerto Rico, at least, these steps worked.

The major step was the king's approval of the *Real Cedula de Gracias* in 1815. This was a set of laws that greatly improved the trade situation in Puerto Rico by expanding foreign trade to any port where there was a Spanish diplomatic office, so long as the trade was on a Spanish ship. It opened the island to immigration by people of any nation so long as they were Roman Catholics and swore allegiance to the king of Spain. New immigrants were given free land (up to six acres per person) and were freed from taxes for a certain number of years so long as they developed the land that they had been given.

Puerto Rico's population was already increasing rapidly. There were many in the South American countries who were faithful to Spain and disapproved of the revolutions there. They were no longer safe in their homelands, and many moved to Puerto Rico. Since these people were all loyal to the king and had usually come from the rich and powerful parts of society, they added to the king's support in Puerto Rico.

Between the flights from revolution and the new immigrants encouraged by free land and no taxes, the population of Puerto Rico quickly grew by more than 30 percent, from one hundred seventy thousand in 1803 to two hundred twenty thousand in 1814. The *Real Cedula* would lead to even more growth.

A true Puerto Rican culture began to flourish. While it had a strongly Spanish flavor to it, Caribbean musical instruments were used to play new and old songs in open-air concerts. Public *fiestas* were organized around the feast day of the patron saint of each town. Even in peasant farming areas, art was valued and farm workers carved *santos,* crude wooden statues of saints, which are highly valued today. A new prosperity came at the same time. People were able to afford better housing and better household goods. The wealthy built their houses of brick instead of wood and had beautiful ironwork balconies and Spanish tile roofs.

Puerto Rican prosperity came also because of the revolutions in the Carribean islands. Haiti had been the major sugar producer. The black revolt on the island destroyed the sugar industry there. The revolts on the mainland also slowed the shipment of items from those countries that were needed in Europe.

At the same time, there was a growing European demand for coffee. Puerto Rico responded by doubling its coffee production in a decade. Increased markets and a better-organized economy meant prosperity. But much of that prosperity was built on the backs of slaves. Puerto Rico continued in the slave trade for many years after it had been forbidden by the Anglo-Spanish Treaty of 1817. Its large sugar plantations depended upon hand labor, as did the coffee plantations. Spaniards had a tradition of not working with their hands, and slaves were cheap labor. There were more than fifty thousand slaves in Puerto Rico, or nearly a fourth of the whole population.

While increased prosperity and freedom and a wave of royal supporters moving to Puerto Rico kept the island under Spanish control, there was some force applied as well. In 1823, Miguel de la Torre was made captain-general. He was to serve for fifteen years in that office and thus become the longest-reigning ruler in Puerto Rico's history. He was a veteran of the king's army in Venezuela, and he was determined that he would not let this colony slip away.

He established a network of spies around the island and built up a military force of more than ten thousand men. This army was not meant just to control the islanders. There was real danger from outside the island as well.

The revolutionaries in South America were anxious to have Puerto Rico join the fold. They wanted to export their newfound freedom, and they wanted to end Puerto Rico's role as the supply base for Spanish armies in South America. They had supporters on the island. A small revolt had taken place in the city of San German in 1811. In 1817, an attack was launched from Buenos Aires in which American sailors were active participants as well. During much of the revolutionary period, there were attempts by the revolutionaries to blockade Puerto Rico to prevent supplies from reaching the Spanish forces.

But, on balance, the island remained relatively calm during these years. The ties to Spain had been strong and grew stronger. The *Creoles* were militarily weak and felt dependent on Spain because they were fearful of a slave revolt such as the one that had destroyed much of Haiti. The people were more prosperous than they had ever been. The reforms of the *Cortes* and the king were not much, but they were enough to provide a reason for hope, especially after the Constitution of 1812.

For whatever reason or combination of reasons, Puerto Rico remained a colony of Spain, as did its neighbor Cuba. But the freedom found on the mainland was not lost on the Puerto Rican people. Spain and Russia were the last absolute monarchies of any size left in Europe. They had outlived their times. Over the coming decades, the Spanish government would rule Puerto Rico rigidly and, in the end, it would pay the price for such rule. For while Puerto Rico may have remained loyal during the great revolutions of the early 1800s, by the end of the century its people had had enough of Spanish dominance.

The process of change took place slowly and quietly and, in the end, it was cut short just at the moment when it seemed that victory had been won. But the effects of the changes during these years would become a major part of the problems presented in modern-day Puerto Rico.

# 6

# The Dawn and Dusk of Independence

*The remainder of the 1800s was a period of broken promises* in Puerto Rico. In 1833, Puerto Rico was granted two seats in the Spanish parliament, and in 1836 those seats were taken away with the promise that this loss would be replaced by greater home rule. That promise remained unkept for sixty years.

Important events were taking place on the international scene, and Puerto Rico was largely ignored from the 1830s through the 1860s. In 1848, a wave of revolutions swept through Europe, changing the governments in many European countries and unsettling the rest. In 1861, civil war broke out in the United States, and for four years this struggle was the focus of interest in the New World.

During this time, Puerto Rican leaders, Cuban leaders, and their allies in Spain itself quietly pressed for more freedom for the Spanish colonies. In 1865, the Spanish government proposed a meeting to discuss laws that would lead to greater autonomy. Puerto Rico elected six delegates to attend that meeting. Three of these were liberals who favored the maximum amount of liberty for Puerto Rico. The other three were conservatives who favored remaining strongly tied to Spain. Two of the three conservatives did not make the trip to Madrid when the meeting began in October of 1866.

The meeting produced several reports. One proposed a bill for the abolition of slavery in Puerto Rico. Puerto Rico stood out among the Caribbean colonies in the number of slaves who had been freed. In 1827, there were four times as many free Africans in Puerto Rico as there were slaves. In every other Caribbean island, the slaves outnumbered the former slaves many times over. The reasons for this difference are not entirely clear. One factor certainly was that the *creole* landowners were often very liberal in their thinking, and to many of them slavery was not acceptable. They freed their own slaves, and, as they grew in power and wealth, the number of freed slaves increased as well.

The Cubans opposed the proposal to free the slaves. Slavery was the major force behind the sugar industry on that island, and slave revolts were fairly common there. The Cubans did not want the message of freedom to spread into their land.

A second report, on which the colonists all agreed, called for the same type of economic reforms that Puerto Ricans had been seeking for two centuries—the right to trade with anyone they pleased, a reduction in tariffs on goods shipped to and from the colonies, and free passage for any ships that wished to come to the colonies to trade.

The third report dealt with political rights, and like the others it included familiar ideas. The colonists sought greater political independence from Spain. They wished to live and be treated in the same way that Spaniards in Spain lived and were treated. They did not elect their most important leaders and they did not have a voice in choosing the leaders in Spain responsible for selecting the leaders of Puerto Rico.

The meeting concluded in April of 1867 amid promises that the reports would be dealt with quickly. They were not dealt with at all, and the reaction in Puerto Rico was swift and violent.

Between September and October of 1868, three different revolts broke out in the Spanish world. The first was the *Gloriosa*. This started in Spain as a military revolt against Queen Isabella II. The Spanish military had grown tired of what it felt was the incompetent rule of the queen. The admiral in charge of the fleet at the Spanish port of Cadiz issued a proclamation calling on other military leaders to join him in revolt. Many quickly agreed to do so, but just as quickly Isabella decided that the throne was not worth fighting for and went into exile in France. This event began five years of chaos in Spain, which led to a further breakdown in Spanish control of the colonies.

The second revolt took place in Puerto Rico itself. Dr. Ramon Emeterio Betances was a physician and an outspoken advocate of Puerto Rican independence. He had been expelled from Puerto Rico by the governor in 1867. Betances settled first in the United States and then moved around various Caribbean islands. He formed alliances with other exiles and some people still in Puerto Rico. These people were not only interested in personal freedom. Many were wealthy landowners who felt that there was too much Spanish control over their property, as well.

In 1868, Betances issued the Ten Commandments of Freedom. He called for the kind of rights for Puerto Ricans that are guaranteed under the American Bill of Rights. He urged freedom of speech and religion, an end to slavery, and economic freedom. In September of 1868, he and his associates moved from words to actions. Hundreds of Betances's supporters took over the town of Lares. When they sought to move on to take the nearby city of San Sebastian, they were quickly defeated by the better-trained and better-armed Spanish troops.

The Lares revolt ended quickly and decisively. The Spanish government was lenient with the revolutionaries. Betances went into exile in France, where he died in 1898. The others were pardoned by the crown. The Lares revolt was never more than a symbol; it had never been a serious threat to Spanish rule. But as a symbol, it was important. Puerto Ricans were growing increasingly unhappy with Spanish rule, and the problem was not going to go away.

A similar situation existed in Cuba. And in October of 1868, a revolt called *El Grito de Yara* broke out. This revolt was to last for ten years of often bitter fighting. In the end, Spain won, but it would not forget the price. From then on, Spain was even more determined to keep a tight rein on its colonies and even less interested in spreading liberty in Puerto Rico.

One positive result of the *Gloriosa* revolt in Spain was that the new government restored representation in the Spanish legislature to Puerto Rico. The Puerto Rican delegates urged the new government to propose new laws governing the relationship between the two. The government agreed, and the proposals took the form of a set of laws that would have led to union between Spain and Puerto Rico, with Puerto Ricans receiving all the rights of Spanish citizens and greater home rule. But there was great opposition to this proposal from other Spanish political groups who were not prepared to see Spain's few remaining colonies drift away from Spanish control. The opposition became so great that the government had to resign, and so another hope for reform in Puerto Rico ended. The one lasting good that came from the short-lived reform period was that the Spanish government did at last end slavery in Puerto Rico in 1873. At that time, nearly thirty-two thousand slaves received their freedom.

After the failure of the Lares revolt, politics became organized in Puerto Rico. Prior to 1870, there were no real political parties as we know them. There were groups who joined together for a common purpose, but they did not last very long, and their agenda was usually limited.

The first political party was the Liberal Reformist party. Their goals were greater home rule in Puerto Rico and political union with Spain. The second party had the confusing name of the Liberal Conservative party. It had the goal of keeping things exactly as they were. For this reason, it received the nickname *Incondicionales,* or the Unconditionals, because its members would not even discuss change in the way that Puerto Rico was governed.

The Liberal Reformist party was by far the more popular one at first. But the Spanish government threw its weight behind the Liberal Conservative party and helped it greatly. One method of doing this was to limit the number of people who were allowed to vote to those who had been born in Spain. These people were by far the most conservative members of Puerto Rican society. By 1880, the laws on voting were so restrictive that only two thousand people out of three hundred seventy-five thousand had the right to vote in elections in Puerto Rico.

The Reformist party was also hurt by a split in its ranks. Many members strongly supported union with Spain. Others wished to see an independent Puerto Rico, perhaps with some ties to Spain, but basically a free nation. They used as their model Canada, which had recently become a dominion of Great Britain. While to us Canada may always have seemed to be a completely independent nation, in fact it was politically bound to Great Britain until the late 1980s when it declared control over its own constitution.

To those who wanted an independent Puerto Rico, the Canadian model was the best of both worlds. It promised the advantages of association with one of the leading nations of Europe and the virtue of real freedom of choice at home. The leader of this group, called the autonomists, was Roman Baldorioty de Castro. He wrote and spoke of his plan, which emphasized human rights, all over Puerto

Rico. He was able to convince many other reformists to join him, and then he campaigned to have the party adopt his program as its platform.

But not everyone in the party agreed with Baldorioty. In a meeting in 1887, the autonomists prevailed. The Reform party became the *Partido Autonomista Puertorriqueno*, or the Puerto Rican Autonomist party. The colonial government was not pleased with this new party and the idea of independence. The governor encouraged a terror campaign against the leaders of the party, and many of them went into exile or prison.

The more moderate members of the Reform party had a different method to reach their goals. Instead of going begging to Madrid to ask for reforms from the Spanish government, they sought to make alliances with Spanish parties.

The leader of this movement was a newspaper editor named Luis Muñoz Rivera. His name is among the most famous in all of Puerto Rican history. He and his son, Luis Muñoz Marín, were to be the major political leaders of Puerto Rico for nearly eighty years. Their names are linked by similarity and by history, but they were in serious political disagreement. Indeed, the son was to spend his adult life away from Puerto Rico until his father died.

Muñoz Rivera* was born in 1859. As a young man, he

*Spanish names can sometimes be confusing to English-speaking readers. Two "last" names are used. The first is the father's family name. The second is the mother's family name. In conversation or in writing, one would refer to Luis Muñoz Marín as Muñoz Marín or Muñoz, never as Marín. Married women traditionally added their husband's family name preceded by de (of), as in Maria

had run for the legislature in Puerto Rico and then, in 1889, founded the newspaper *La Democracia.* While Muñoz Marín will forever be known for his political activities, he was also the author of two books of poetry, *Retamas* in 1891 and *Tropicales* in 1902.

Muñoz Rivera proposed that the autonomists form an alliance with the Spanish Fusionist party, a party that supported the monarchy in Spain. Muñoz Rivera reasoned that if the Puerto Ricans were going to join forces with a Spanish political party, it might as well be one that had a chance of coming to power in Spain, and a monarchist party seemed to be the type that would control the Spanish government.

This decision may have been very practical, but it caused a good deal of upset. Many Puerto Ricans who did not object to union with Spain believed in democracy and opposed monarchy. So the Reformists were split even further by this proposal. The dispute about what party to support lingered on for years. Finally, in 1896, a commission of party members was sent to Madrid to work out an agreement with a Spanish party that would support an independent status for Puerto Rico.

By early 1897, the commission had reached an agreement with the Fusionist party that called for a union of the Spanish and Puerto Rican branches of the party. It did not call for an independent Puerto Rico as much as it pointed toward a Puerto Rico with increased home rule

---

Gonzalez de Rivera. *Since the de implies ownership by the husband, this is dying out.*

but continuing strong ties with Spain. This agreement led to a permanent split in the reform movement, and two new parties emerged. The first, led by Muñoz Rivera, was the Liberal Fusionist party, the branch of the Spanish party called for in the agreement. The second, led by Dr. Jose Celso Barbosa, called itself the Orthodox Historical Autonomist party.

In the meantime, revolt had broken out in Cuba again. Tension about the Caribbean colonies reached a new height. Then there was a sudden change in the Spanish government. The prime minister of Spain was assassinated, and the Spanish Fusionist party took control in August of 1897.

Within ninety days, the new government had issued a set of decrees to grant significant local independence to Puerto Rico. Its people were to be granted the same rights as Spanish citizens, and local control of the government was to be greatly but not completely expanded. Spain would still appoint a governor who would retain enormous power. He would appoint all judges, control the budget, and appoint half of the members of one house of the legislature. But individual liberties were to be greatly expanded. The people of the island were given control over who could vote in elections. Their elected representatives controlled the education system and approved local taxes and budgets.

The Autonomic Charter, as it was known, was not a perfect document, but it was an enormous change from pure colonialism. Before it could go into effect, though, the Spanish government required that the two Reformist factions get together. This was not easily accomplished. Barbosa and Muñoz Rivera were both proud, and both wished to lead the new government. They did come to an agreement and then broke it before the elections under the charter took place. Muñoz Rivera triumphed easily in those elections, and the new government prepared to take office in May of 1898.

However, war had broken out between Spain and the United States, and the legislature did not meet until July 17, 1898. This was the first day of a truly Puerto Rican government. On July 25, the United States invaded Puerto Rico.

# 7

# An American Colony

*This is not a book about Spain or the United States, but about* Puerto Rico. So, for our purposes, the Spanish-American War is important because it changed Puerto Rico from a Spanish colony with the first signs of independence to an American colony under military rule.

The United States had long been protected by its oceans, content to leave alone and be left alone by the rest of the world. But several things happened in the second half of the nineteenth century to change that. The United States had grown enormously in population and wealth. In numbers and in power, it was now among the strongest nations of the world. The full development of the ironclad steamship meant that powerful ships could move quickly across the ocean to the United States. The United States had conquered its frontier. All the territory in today's fifty states was part of the United States, and all but a handful of these states had already joined the Union. Finally, imperialism, the forceful taking of another's territory, had become politically acceptable around the world.

The United States was afraid for its safety because its

ocean borders were no longer a protection from Europe's wars. But the United States was also at full strength. It was anxious to take its place among the world's great powers and had nowhere in its own territory to test out its strength. Spain, on the other hand, was a declining power. Its government was in chaos. Its prime minister had just been assassinated, and its political parties had just gone through drastic changes. It possessed Puerto Rico and Cuba, two islands that would be useful in defending a canal across Central America. Such a canal was the dream of the United States because it would make ocean travel from the East Coast to the West Coast easier and quicker than the long trip around Cape Horn at the southern tip of South America.

When the American battleship *Maine* was blown up in Havana Harbor, the United States went to war with Spain. There has always been a debate about how the ship came to explode, but we shall not enter that debate. The explosion provided a convenient reason for the United States to do what it had long wanted to do—go to war with Spain and take its territories by force.

The war began on April 19, 1898. The first action in Puerto Rico came less than a month later. An American fleet looking for a Spanish fleet sailed into San Juan Harbor. The Spanish fleet was not there, but the seven American ships under the command of Admiral William Sampson fired on the centuries-old wall surrounding San Juan. The Spanish guns along the walls fired back. Very little damage was done by either side, and the American fleet soon sailed away.

In July, though, the Americans came to stay. On the

twenty-fifth of that month, an American fleet entered the Bay of Guánica, and a landing party raised the American flag. This small group was soon joined by more than three thousand other American troops. The Americans had landed on Puerto Rico's southern coast because of reports that people in that region were unhappy with Spanish rule. The reports were correct, and the Americans were greeted warmly. They fanned out on the island, and by the time Spain surrendered only three weeks later, the United States controlled Puerto Rico.

They found an island that had grown greatly during the nineteenth century. The population was nearly one million people, and it was more thickly populated than the state of Pennsylvania.

A majority of the population was European, but nearly 40 percent were of African, Indian, or mixed-race origin. The economy was agricultural, with coffee and sugar the leading crops. Nearly all of the farms were worked by their owners as compared with other islands, such as Cuba, where most of the farms were owned by landlords who lived in other places and whose only interest was in how much profit the land could make for them.

The Puerto Ricans welcomed the Americans for a strange mix of reasons. Even those, such as Muñoz Rivera, who had sought a union with Spain did not do so out of love for Spain. They saw such a union as their one route to individual rights. They were not so much concerned with which nation governed them, as that it governed them fairly.

Many Puerto Ricans admired the United States. The

United States had aided Cuban revolutionaries, though its reasons may have been selfish ones. The United States was seen by many as a nation that supported liberty and would do so in Puerto Rico. The main supporters of the Spanish government were native-born Spaniards living in Puerto Rico. Many of these returned to Spain.

Some Puerto Ricans, though, were distrustful of the United States. Muñoz Rivera himself considered opposing the invading Americans with force, but he decided that he would stand little chance in such a struggle.

So the American era in Puerto Rico began with good feeling. While some were certainly disappointed that the Americans had arrived just when Puerto Ricans had achieved a measure of control in their own lives, still they held forth great hope that the interruption in progress would be temporary. A few years of American occupation would be followed by genuine independence or perhaps statehood, they thought. That, actually, was the American plan for Cuba, which had also been taken during the war.

In fact, for most people, it seems that their ideas about Puerto Rico's status had not changed very much at all. They had been prepared to accept political union with Spain if that was easier to achieve than pure independence. They were prepared to accept political union (statehood) with the United States for the same reasons.

The American colonial administrators were military people at first. They, of course, had no particular interest in the long-term political fate of the island. Their interest was in preserving Puerto Rico as a territory of the United

States and as the fortress guarding the Caribbean. Their actions were designed to enhance that control. In letters to Washington, they spoke of the Puerto Rican people as "children," unready to bear the burdens of democracy. They took firm control of virtually every aspect of Puerto Rican life. Puerto Ricans had less freedom than they had had under Spanish rule. Local governments were disbanded, newspapers were forced to stop publishing, and the military leaders took control over all major economic decisions.

The Puerto Ricans suffered economically too. American tobacco and sugar interests worked to cut off Puerto Rican competition by getting the American government to impose a high tariff on those items from Puerto Rico. Then, in 1899, a tremendous hurricane known as *San Ciriaco* hit Puerto Rico, totally destroying the coffee crop and ruining many of the coffee trees. Puerto Rico's three main crops were either gone or had lost much of their market.

The martial law did not last very long, although military people were to remain important in the Puerto Rican government for many years to come. In April of 1900, Congress passed the Foraker Act. It was to stay in effect for seventeen years. It provided for an elected house of representatives, but the governor was to be from the American military and he would have the major share of the political power on the island. The American sugar and tobacco interests had provisions included that put a heavy tariff on Puerto Rican goods for at least two years.

Many Americans felt that the Foraker Act was far too

severe. The act was tested in the courts in what became known as the Insular Cases. The United States Supreme Court ruled that Congress could set up territories the way it had with Puerto Rico, Cuba, and the Philippines. The Foraker Act structure was not intended to be a pathway to statehood, and some members of the Court felt that this was improper, arguing that the Constitution did not permit Congress to set up territories that belonged to but were not a part of the United States.

Puerto Rican reaction was angry. Muñoz Rivera, who was by then the leading politician on the island, wrote to President McKinley, stating that the Foraker Act was "unworthy of the United States which imposes it and of the Puerto Ricans who have to endure it." But neither Muñoz Rivera nor any other Puerto Rican had the political strength in the United States to change things. The act did bring the warring political parties in Puerto Rico together, though. They formed the Unionist party, which was willing to support any of three options. It would accept statehood, true nationhood, or semi-independence under American protection.

The Foraker Act lasted until World War I was well under way. The main thrust of American efforts in those years was economic improvement, Americanization, and what is known as tutelage. *Tutelage* was a word used to express what Americans felt was needed in Puerto Rico— training its people in how to behave as a civilized nation. It expressed the attitude that the American way was the only right way. Because it was right for Americans, it was right for everyone.

The economy did improve greatly. Trade with the United States grew fourfold in ten years. Americanization was carried out in the schools. Then as now, Puerto Rico had only one school system. There is not a different school board in each city or town. All of the schools are run by the commonwealth government. In seven years, the number of students attending those schools nearly tripled. One object of this program was bilingualism, having the people speak English as well as Spanish. The language issue is a crucial one to this day.

Tutelage involved training for democracy. The American government was looking for signs that the people were ready for self-government. Such things as literacy rates were supposed to be important in this judgment. But the notes and letters of the American governors suggest something else was being sought. They were waiting for the Puerto Rican people to be just like them, to share their attitudes and beliefs. They recognized that Puerto Rico was a different culture, and because it was different, they thought it was inferior.

Such a view was foolish but not surprising. The United States was an isolated nation with very little experience with the differing cultures around it. It was also a young nation that had grown very strong. Americans felt that they were blessed, as they were, with economic strength and a strong belief in liberty. From these strengths, they concluded that not only was their way the right way, but also that it was the only right way.

Congressional leaders and even federal judges were to speak of Puerto Rico and its people in terms such as "childish." But terms like "mongrel race" and "Latin American talkers" were also heard. This was a time when the fear of other cultures was at one of its high points in the United States. The Ku Klux Klan was strong, and prejudice against Asians was rampant. The racist views were probably not representative of the views of all Americans, but they were held by people in positions of great influence over Puerto Rico.

Against this background, Muñoz Rivera was working quietly to change things. In 1910, he moved to Washington as Puerto Rico's representative to Congress. For six years, he worked to change the Foraker Act. In the sixth year, he died. In the seventh year, the act was replaced.

Congress had been considering new legislation several years before that time. Independence was not an issue in Congress. Puerto Rico was too important to national defense, now that the Panama Canal had been opened, and the Americans stuck to the view that the Puerto Rican people were not able to govern themselves. In addition, by this time American sugar companies had invested heavily in Puerto Rico. They did not want to take a chance at losing that investment.

The real issue was citizenship. For the Unionist party, citizenship was a two-edged sword. On the one hand, it meant that Puerto Rican citizens would have many of the same legal rights as persons in the United States. On the other hand, it meant an acceptance, though the Unionists denied this, of continuing American control of Puerto Rico because accepting American citizenship seemed to mean accepting a permanent relationship with the United

States. Should they accept greater rights at the risk of losing the chance of future independence?

People were divided over the issue in the United States too. Those who looked down on the Puerto Rican people opposed citizenship. Those who respected them had the same concern the Unionists did—that citizenship might mean an end to the possibility of independence.

Some Puerto Ricans, particularly Santiago Iglesias, who was the leading labor leader in Puerto Rico, were willing to trade away the political rights involved in citizenship for greater economic rights such as minimum wage laws.

World War I ended the confusion on this issue. By 1917, the United States was preparing to enter that war. That meant that the Panama Canal would become a target for the Germans. Puerto Rico was an important defense post for the canal, but the Virgin Islands were an even better point for protection of the canal. The United States purchased those islands from Denmark in 1917, but, as part of the treaty selling the islands, Denmark insisted on American citizenship for all of the inhabitants who wanted it. Congress had the Puerto Rican citizenship question before it at the same time. It would have been a gross injustice to grant citizenship to these new possessions and not to the Puerto Ricans, who had been a part of the United States for almost twenty years. This ended the question of citizenship. The Jones Act, as the new legislation was called, granted American citizenship to the Puerto Rican people.

The Jones Act contained some advances for the Puerto

Rican people too. Both houses of the legislature would be elected for the first time. Up to that point, the senate had been made up of appointed persons. Some important administrative posts would have to be approved by the Puerto Rican Senate, so the Puerto Ricans had some veto power over the choices of their American governor. But none of these rights was guaranteed forever. Every right that Puerto Ricans had could be changed by Congress because Congress had given the right.

But many Puerto Ricans saw the Jones Act as a sign of good faith on the part of the United States, another step on the road to self-government. This support can be measured in Puerto Rican reaction to the United States's entry into World War I. Nearly twenty thousand Puerto Ricans served in the armed forces of the United States during the war, and the Puerto Rican people donated hundreds of thousands of dollars to the Red Cross and bought over $10 million in war bonds.

No one thought that the Jones Act was the final word on the status of Puerto Rico. Everyone knew that the question of statehood or independence in some form would have to be faced someday. But the nation was at war, and the strategic importance of Puerto Rico was too great to be ignored at this point. The big decision would be made somewhere down the road.

*Albizu Campos and other Nationalists on trial for rebellion in 1936*

*This picture of San Juan in the 1930s shows the mixture of Spanish and English that Americanization brought about.*

*Albizu supporters outside Nationalist party headquarters after the Ponce Massacre in 1937*

*The depression destroyed an already fragile Puerto Rican economy, but broader education was creating a hope for the future.*

*Rexford Tugwell (on the stairs) was a member of Franklin Roosevelt's "brain trust" and the depression-era governor of Puerto Rico.*

*Luis Muñoz Marín (with mustache) was at home in the countryside and in the highest offices in San Juan and in Washington, D.C.*

# 8

# A New Commonwealth

*The war and the Jones Act brought a new era to Puerto Rico.* Within a short time after the war's end, Barbosa and Muñoz Rivera were both dead. A new generation of leaders would shortly emerge. For some years, the fragile Unionist party held together just enough to win elections in Puerto Rico by narrow margins. But the prostatehood Socialist party, led by the charismatic labor leader Santiago Iglesias and supported by American trade unions, was gaining ground rapidly on the old party. Iglesias's issues were the economy and the tyranny of the sugar industry, which was largely controlled by non–Puerto Ricans.

In other areas, though, Puerto Ricans were gaining more control of their society. President Wilson had appointed Arthur Yager as governor in 1913, and Yager had stayed for eight years, the longest term ever for an appointed governor. He had a strong policy of appointing native Puerto Ricans to government positions, and by the time he left office, only a handful of teachers and other public servants were not Puerto Ricans.

But Wilson left office in 1921, and so did Yager. President Harding used the open governor's position to reward an old friend, E. Montgomery Reily. Reily knew little about Puerto Rico and even less about how government operated. His goal was to make Puerto Rico just like home. He did not understand the distinct, centuries-old culture of the island. If Puerto Rico was to be a permanent part of the United States, as he was sure it should be, its language should be English and its customs should be American. He treated Puerto Rico as if it were his own personal kingdom. Fortunately, his reign was short. He was indicted for misusing public funds in Puerto Rico and was forced to resign.

But Reily was not just a problem himself, he was also a symptom of a larger problem. After twenty-five years of controlling Puerto Rico, Americans were treating it as if it was and always would be a part of the United States. Cuba had been let go shortly after the Spanish-American War, and the Philippines would be granted freedom in due course. The United States regarded these two areas as both more ready for self-government and less important to the defense of the United States. But the idea of independence for Puerto Rico was becoming more and more remote.

The autonomists, who had earlier found some hope in the Canadian model, now looked at the Irish model. Southern Ireland had lately been freed from British control. There were some economic and political connections, but basically it was a free nation, known as the Irish

Free State. The autonomists began to discuss the idea of what was called the *Estado Libre Asociado,* the free associated state. As the title implies, under this model Puerto Rico would be a free nation with some associations, political and economic, with the United States.

But this was not a good era for discussing disconnecting from the United States. The memory of Puerto Rico's wartime value was too clear, and a new president, Calvin Coolidge, had replaced Harding, who had died in office. He was not interested in the issue. A Unionist effort to gain the right to elect a governor had failed, and the economic issues in Puerto Rico were uppermost in the minds of many people.

After the defeat on the governorship issue, many Puerto Ricans who supported statehood realized that *their* dream too would have to be delayed. If the Congress would not allow the people to elect their own governor, it certainly would not invite Puerto Rico to join the union as a state.

With both independence and statehood cut off as options, the concept of a free associated state grew more attractive. Both the statehood supporters and the independence supporters were also concerned about the growing power of the Socialists. That party was not much concerned about the status issue. Its concerns were economic. If the statehooders and the independence advocates split the vote of those to whom status was the most important issue, then the Socialists would win control of the government.

The leaders of the two groups formed a new political

coalition called the *Alianza*. Some statehood supporters, who felt that the new group had abandoned the basic issue of status, joined forces with the Socialists to form the *Coalicion* (Coalition). The *Alianza* was much the stronger of the two and took the place of the Unionists as the major political party in Puerto Rico.

With the status question temporarily put aside, the focus on economics became even sharper. Puerto Rico was a source of riches for American companies, particularly sugar companies. Three such companies controlled nearly half of the sugar crop. Taxes were low, and so were wages, but profits were high. The wealth of Puerto Rico was in its agriculture, and that wealth was leaving Puerto Rico on ships bound for the United States.

Horace Towner of Iowa had replaced Reily as governor, and he was a much more thoughtful man. While he was no champion of Puerto Rican culture, he was genuinely interested in the well-being of the island and of its people. He had been a member of Congress and had been a leader in the passage of the Jones Act. He supported changes in the tax structure that would keep some of Puerto Rico's wealth for the use of its own people. The president who appointed him, Coolidge, sounded much more like Reily. Upon receiving a request from the Puerto Rican political leaders asking him to consider greater home rule for Puerto Rico, he responded by announcing that Puerto Ricans should consider themselves lucky to have the freedom that they did have.

The next Republican president, Herbert Hoover, was far better for Puerto Rico. His appointment as governor was Theodore Roosevelt, Jr., son of the former president, who turned his attention to Puerto Rico with all of his family's well-known energy. He read all he could on the island and its history and learned to speak Spanish. By that time, Puerto Rico was in great need of attention. In 1928, the coffee and cane industries had once more been devastated by a major hurricane, during which two hundred fifty thousand houses were destroyed. One commentator described Puerto Rico as the "poorhouse of the Caribbean."

Roosevelt rejected "the hopeless drive to remodel Puerto Ricans so that they should become similar in language, habits and thoughts to continental Americans." His efforts were devoted to making Puerto Rico an economically independent place. His concern was supported by the American "think tank," the Brookings Institution, which in 1930 issued a report showing in great detail the horrible state of the Puerto Rican economy.

While Roosevelt may have had the right idea as to the problem, he did not have any great answers to it and he stayed only two years. Moreover, Roosevelt had the attitude that many other Americans had toward Puerto Rico. Though he believed that Puerto Rico should keep its own cultural identity, he seemed to think that the very culture he was in favor of keeping was inferior, not just different.

His cousin Franklin Roosevelt became president in 1933. FDR's early attitudes toward Puerto Rico showed concern but no real understanding. It was his wife, Eleanor Roosevelt, who visited Puerto Rico to see not its grand buildings but its poor farms. She became friends with Luis Muñoz Marín, the son of Muñoz Rivera.

Muñoz Marín was born in 1898, the year that Puerto Rico was captured by the United States. He was a child of the American era just as his father had been a child of the Spanish era. He was an intellectual who was devoted to the interests of the poorest of Puerto Ricans, and also a skilled politician who spent many years in Washington and New York.

Muñoz Marín left Puerto Rico as a teenager. He went to high school and college in Washington and was attending law school in that city when his father died. He abruptly abandoned legal studies and moved to New York City, where he became a writer like his wife, the Mississippi-born poet Muna Lee.

Muñoz Marín wrote mostly for what were liberal magazines such as the *New Republic* and the *Nation*. He also translated a number of books, including those of Walt Whitman, into Spanish. He had become a popular and well-respected intellectual in the United States.

But Muñoz Marín had a foot in each world. He grew up and was educated in the United States. He was married to an American. He was a well-known writer in major American publications. But he was also the editor of the Latin American cultural journal *La Revista de Indias*. And his heart was in Puerto Rico. In particular, he had a deep and lifelong concern for the *jibaros*, the peasant farmers and workers there.

His father had seen his role as global. He played international politics, negotiating with Spain and the United States. The son knew that the status issue was an important one, but the issue closest to his heart was that of the lives of the poor. This difference in emphasis divided father and son, and Muñoz Marín was said to have spoken of his father only as a historical figure.

Ten years after his father's death in 1916, Muñoz Marín returned to Puerto Rico to edit his father's paper, *La Democracia,* and was elected to the Puerto Rican Senate in 1932, the same year that Roosevelt was elected president.

It was a difficult time because the Great Depression, the worst economic catastrophe of the century in the Western world, had hit Puerto Rico hard, as we shall see. Puerto Rico needed help, and Washington was the only place it could look to.

Though Muñoz Marín's political career had just begun, his influence in Washington was greater than that of any other Puerto Rican, perhaps because he had lived in that city for so long. He was to use that influence with great skill. He was to become the first elected governor of Puerto Rico and was to be reelected three more times. He might well have served in the office until his death in 1980 but, in 1964, he chose to take a seat in the Puerto Rican Senate and let another take his place as governor. This was a great act of statesmanship, placing the interests of the people of Puerto Rico above his own interests.

While Franklin Roosevelt was learning from Eleanor Roosevelt about Puerto Rico, his first decision about the island was a very bad one. His nominee for governor was Robert Gore. Gore was no more than a local politician, and his idea of reform in Puerto Rico was to make sure that all the important jobs were held by Democrats. At that time and even up to this day, the Democratic and Republican parties have no serious existence in Puerto Rico. The local parties have always been far more important than the national ones. Muñoz Marín used his influence to have Gore removed as governor.

Muñoz Marín was able to have increasing influence over Roosevelt's policies toward Puerto Rico. Roosevelt's reform programs in the United States went by the name the New Deal. But much of the New Deal policies had no particular role in Puerto Rico. They were often aimed at restoring the health of industry, and Puerto Rico had very little industry at that time.

Economic conditions in Puerto Rico had been worse than on the mainland before the depression. The depression turned a bad situation into a disaster. The daily life of the people in Puerto Rico, especially rural Puerto Rico where most of the population then lived, was terrible even by the standards of the Great Depression.

In the mid-1930s, a worker in the sugar fields of Puerto Rico earned around $120 a year. Factory workers in the city fared better. They made $5 a week, more than double the wage of the sugar workers. Few farmers owned their own land. Over the years, the giant sugar companies had gained control over more and more of the plantable land, and only 20 percent was owned by the people who worked it.

More than half of the children did not wear shoes. The lack of shoes meant that hookworms, which enter the body through cuts in the feet, were common. In rural

Puerto Rico, 83 percent of the people had hookworms. Dental care was almost nonexistent. About one in seven people had nine or more teeth missing.

Less than half the children went to school, and half of those went only part of the day. There were no high schools in rural Puerto Rico, and those people who went to school rarely went beyond the fourth grade. These numbers are more than fifty years old, and that is a long time ago. But the children that these numbers help to describe are just reaching retirement age now. So the problems that poor education and poor medical care caused are still being felt in Puerto Rico today.

The increasing poverty and the sense of hopelessness about the status and economic issues led to greater popularity for the more radical political parties. Such parties have always been active and visible in Puerto Rico, although they never have had any real election victories. Chief among these at that time was the Nationalist party. It had been founded in the early 1920s when the major parties in Puerto Rico had, temporarily at least, given up on the idea that the status question could be solved in the near future. But it had remained without any real influence until 1930 when its new leader, Pedro Albizu Campos, injected new life into it.

The terrible economic conditions helped Albizu, because one of the strongest arguments against independence had been that ties with the United States helped Puerto Rico economically. Things were so bad in the 1930s that independence could not be seen as making things worse.

Educated in chemistry and law at Harvard, Albizu had no great liking for the United States. He saw Puerto Rico's future as tied not to the United States, but to the other islands in the Caribbean. When his party did poorly at the polls, Albizu gave up on the idea of winning elections and sought to build a revolutionary movement. He hoped to find allies among the college students, but in a rally at the University of Puerto Rico in 1935, the students protested against him. A group of Nationalists at the rally got into a gun fight with the police. Three Nationalists were killed. In apparent retaliation for these deaths, the chief of police was murdered three months later. The two men who had killed him were, in turn, executed by the police.

A peculiar reaction to these tragic events was a renewed interest, in Washington, in Puerto Rican independence if the people of Puerto Rico voted for it. A bill to that effect was introduced and even had administration support. Some people favored independence as punishment, and some favored independence as a means of resolving the problems that had lead to the bloodshed. But the bill had a catch to it. Within four years after independence, Puerto Rico would pay the same tariffs on goods shipped into the United States that other nations did. For an economy already in ruins, that condition was impossible. Even the strongest advocates of independence realized this, and the bill died without further congressional action.

But the cycle of violence continued. Seventeen Albizu supporters were shot in the city of Ponce on Palm Sunday in 1937. Albizu himself was in jail on charges of attempting to overthrow the federal rule in Puerto Rico by inciting an uprising among the people. The *Coalicion* and *Alianza* parties were breaking up, Muñoz Marín had formed his own independence party, the Popular Democratic party (PPD), and the world seemed ready to go to war again. Progress must have seemed to be impossible.

In 1941, though, President Roosevelt appointed Rexford G. Tugwell as governor of Puerto Rico. Tugwell was an economist who had been a member of FDR's "brain trust." He had visited Puerto Rico and seen its problems firsthand. Tugwell was also a visionary. He saw as much opportunity in Puerto Rico as he saw despair. And by that time, there was some reason for hope.

War in Europe brought prosperity to the island. If Scotch whiskey was not being shipped past German submarines, Puerto Rican rum, made from sugarcane, could be. The war once more drew attention to Puerto Rico's strategic position, and massive sums of money went into strengthening the defenses of the island. That money meant jobs and some industrial development.

In addition, there were social changes. Some of these came about because of Tugwell's attitudes and his friendship with Muñoz Marín. Others came about because the United States did not want to have to rely on Puerto Rico as a fortress while its people were hostile to the United States.

Tugwell's economic plan involved the establishment of "public corporations." These groups—eventually there were fourteen of them—were to be free of active governmental control, and each was assigned an area of the economy to develop. Tugwell chose young Puerto Ricans (at the average age of thirty-one) to run these corporations. The economy of Puerto Rico was to be controlled by the government in a way that had no equal in any part of the United States.

The reaction to Tugwell's plans in Congress was very negative. He was accused of being everything from a Communist to a Fascist. And his plan was not all that successful. But it did represent action and it did give substantial control over the economy back to Puerto Ricans.

Tugwell's support strengthened Muñoz Marín's power. His new party, the PPD, had won a very close election in 1940. By 1944, its majority was overwhelming, and Muñoz Marín was clearly the political leader of Puerto Rico. But while the war continued, there was no chance for movement on the status question.

The war ended in 1945, and Tugwell's time as governor ended in the following year. The end of the war also signaled a change in attitudes. For many Americans, the war represented a struggle against the last gasp of imperialism and colonialism. The war's conclusion saw former colonies throughout the world gaining their independence with the strong support of the United States. It did not take much imagination to have these events bring the subject of Puerto Rico to mind. Those who were not very imaginative were reminded of the similarity by Muñoz Marín. But Muñoz Marín had come to have doubts about complete independence. He was concerned about the economic future of a totally independent Puerto Rico. He had come to favor some formal continuing link with the United States.

Events moved quickly. In 1946, President Truman appointed Jesús T. Piñero as the first Puerto Rican governor of Puerto Rico. In 1947, Congress finally enacted a bill calling for an elected governor in Puerto Rico. The next year, Muñoz Marín became the first Puerto Rican elected to hold that position. After four hundred fifty years, the chief position in the government was held by someone who came from Puerto Rico and had been selected by its people. The PPD had also won great majorities in both houses of the Puerto Rican legislature. Muñoz Marín and his followers were in complete control of the local political structure.

Puerto Rico was making great strides economically as well. The Industrial Incentives Act, passed by the Puerto Rican legislature in 1947, provided freedom from taxes for ten years to new businesses. This program and others, called Operation Bootstrap, combined with the low wages on the island, caused a great deal of investment from American companies and boosted the island's economy significantly. The wealth of Puerto Rico doubled in just over a decade. But there was a price for economic growth. That growth was dependent upon a close political relationship with the United States. If that relationship was broken, the trade barriers would go up, and the investments would go down. So greater economic freedom also meant greater political dependence. The link between economics and political status became stronger.

With the economic situation improving, Muñoz Marín turned his attention to resolving the status dilemma. He had, earlier in his career, rejected the idea of a free associated state, the Irish solution. He regarded it as freedom "on a long chain." But by 1948, he had either changed his mind or found that he had no other choice. "If we seek statehood," he said, "we die waiting for Congress, and if we adopt independence we die from starvation—either way we die." His PPD adopted the concept of an "intermediate solution" and went to Washington to try to achieve it.

The tide was going Muñoz Marín's way. In 1950, Congress passed Public Law 600. This called for an election in Puerto Rico to determine whether the free associated state concept would be adopted. If the voters said yes, then Puerto Ricans would draft a constitution that had to be approved by Congress and could be amended by Congress. The agreement would be one "in the nature of a compact." Advocates of independence and of statehood rejected the idea. If Congress still could control and amend the Puerto Rican constitution, then the independence promised by Public Law 600 was independence only so long as Congress wanted it to be. For statehood supporters, the proposal provided nothing but continued delay in becoming an equal part of the United States.

Muñoz Marín felt differently. It was his view that, once the constitution had been approved by the people of Puerto Rico, it would be a dramatic breach of faith for Congress to interfere with it. While the terms of Public Law 600 did not grant Puerto Rico legal independence, they did give it actual independence, and that was good enough.

The *independentistas,* the more vocal supporters of independence, decided not to participate in the election since it did not give them the choice that they wanted, true independence. Some of them engaged in violent protest. Twenty-seven people were killed during the period before the election. Some of these deaths occurred in an attack on the governor's mansion. But the most dramatic attack was on the president of the United States, Harry S Truman, during which a policeman and an *independentista* were killed. At the same time, other *independentistas* opened fire in the Congress of the United States itself.

Despite these events, the election took place in June of 1951. Two-thirds of the people of Puerto Rico turned out to vote, and by nearly four to one, they approved the new relationship.

A new era had begun in Puerto Rico's relationship with the United States. Puerto Rico was now referred to, in English, as a commonwealth. No one had any particularly clear idea of what a commonwealth was or what changes it would mean in the lives and government of Puerto Rico. But it was a recognition that Puerto Rico was somehow different and that the relationship with the United States was not that of a state, a colony, or an independent nation. The details would be worked out in time, and the relationship would be changed to statehood or independence as events dictated. That, anyway, was the theory.

# 9

# A Continuing Debate

*Muñoz Marín believed that he had established an arrange-*
ment with the United States in which all parties got what
they wanted. In English, the arrangement was called a
commonwealth, a term that has no legal meaning, so that
every American point of view on Puerto Rico's political
status could claim victory. In Spanish, the relationship
was legally described as a free associated state. For those
who favored independence, the word *free* was there. For
those who favored continuing political and economic ties
with the United States, the word *associated* was comfort-
ing. Even those who supported statehood had the word
*state* in the title.

What is clear is that the compact was a unilateral agreement. That is, one party and one party alone—the Congress—could change it. Puerto Rico could propose
changes, but it could not make them. Congress could
probably even make changes over the opposition of the
people of Puerto Rico. The legal relationship was unsatis-
factory to everyone. But to each, it also held open the

possibility that their view would prevail because it was not, or so it seemed at the time, a permanent solution to the status question.

Muñoz Marín saw it as an opening, a path to be followed toward greater self-rule. He quietly organized an effort to "perfect" the commonwealth status. Perfection in this case meant making steady but quiet efforts to achieve greater independence from American controls, to take small parts of Puerto Rican life and have them governed by Puerto Ricans.

But one unforeseen consequence of the commonwealth status was that it became increasingly common for Congress automatically to apply American laws to Puerto Rico. For the most part, such laws have been beneficial to the people of the island, since they have tended to involve social programs. However, such constant additions made the program of perfection quite difficult. It became rather like the old comedy skit in which the worker in a bakery is picking pies up off a conveyor belt and putting them in boxes, when the belt starts to move ever more rapidly. By the end, the worker is unable to keep up with the pies, and pies are splattered all over the room and the worker.

Muñoz Marín's plan for a perfected commonwealth status had another obstacle in front of it. The supporters of statehood would never agree to such a plan, because it made the achievement of statehood less and less likely. If Muñoz Marín succeeded and the island received as much or more freedom than a state did, why should anyone consider statehood? Statehood meant two things to most people—voting representation in Congress and the imposition of federal taxes. Having representation in Congress is good, but the benefits are not immediate. No one, of course, is anxious to pay taxes.

The *independentistas* did not like the idea much either. To them, a perfected commonwealth was like being half-free. Moreover, they knew that if Puerto Rico achieved a substantial measure of local control, then many people would not wish to risk the uncertainty of independence.

In 1959, Munoz Marín felt increasingly frustrated that the status issue had lingered on. In addition, since 1948 the parties supporting statehood had gained an increasing number of votes every year. He decided on a bold stroke. He would seek congressional approval of a plan that would go a long way toward his vision of a perfected commonwealth. Rather than attack the issue a little bit at a time, he would try to achieve most of his plan in one move. Under this plan, Puerto Rico would control much of its own economic structure such as wages, tariffs, and other items. Puerto Rico and the United States would have their relationship controlled by Articles of Permanent Association. These articles could not be amended without the approval of the people of Puerto Rico.

The last item is, of course, the crucial one. The articles would be something very much like a constitution. Instead of a unilateral agreement, this would be a bilateral agreement between two peoples—the Americans and the Puerto Ricans. Neither one could change the agreement by themselves. Both parties would have to be in agreement. This amounted to full sovereignty for Puerto Rico. It would become more independent than any state, since the states cannot control tariffs, and nearly as independent as any nation.

But Muñoz Marín's plan failed. Members of Congress were concerned that it was too radical a change. Statehood supporters in Puerto Rico and the United States were strongly opposed to it. They saw statehood gaining more support every year and they did not want to let Muñoz Marín end the debate when he was losing ground. Employees of the federal government in Puerto Rico saw it as a grave risk to their jobs because they would eventually become Puerto Rican government jobs. Muñoz Marín saw that the bill had no chance of passing and he abandoned it.

But he kept his strong desire to settle the issue once and for all. What he needed was a mechanism to do that. If not legislation, then why not another election?

There was an argument that the 1951 referendum was flawed. In it, the people of Puerto Rico had been offered only one choice. They could accept the commonwealth concept, or they could leave things exactly as they were. The vote, then, can be looked at as a vote for change, any change. In 1951, there were very few people in Puerto Rico who did not feel that a change was needed. So, in voting for change, they were not necessarily truly supporting the idea of a commonwealth relationship with the United States. They were just saying that they did not like what they had and that they were willing to try anything different.

But an election with all choices presented would have much greater legitimacy. In 1963, Muñoz Marín sought such an election. Muñoz Marín knew that Congress would not support or pay attention to an election unless there was a showing that the people of Puerto Rico wanted such an election. The *independentistas* would not support the election because they knew they would lose and because they believed that their loss would come about because of American influence. Statehood supporters would seem to have little to gain from such an election since Muñoz Marín was himself so popular that an election might turn out to be a referendum on him and not on the issues. But he was able to persuade them to support the idea for a while. When they realized that the commonwealth option Muñoz Marín proposed was not just a temporary continuation of the present commonwealth, but a permanent status that effectively ended the idea of statehood, they wanted no part of it. Without their support, there would be no congressional support, and the idea of an election died.

There would be no perfecting legislation and there would be no election. There was a third way to attempt to bring matters to a head, and that was a commission. In 1964, the United States–Puerto Rico Commission on the Status of Puerto Rico began its work. It was chaired by James A. Rowe, Jr., who was familiar with Puerto Rican society and government. The commission worked for two years and produced an extraordinary record. But its conclusion was not very helpful. It decided that every option was a legitimate one and that it was up to the people of Puerto Rico to decide what they wanted.

The commission did point out that if independence

were the choice, a fifteen-year transition period would be needed to smooth the way economically. It also pointed out that statehood would also be hard on the Puerto Rican economy. At that time, the increased burden of federal taxation would cost the people of Puerto Rico $188 million. Each path was difficult, and one, the perfected commonwealth, was untried.

This time it was clear that a referendum would take place, and that possibility tore the political parties in Puerto Rico apart. In Muñoz Marín's PPD, there were many who saw commonwealth status as just a stop on the path to independence. Since the election would include permanent, perfected commonwealth status as an option, they opposed it. Most statehood supporters were in the Puerto Rican Republican party (PER), and many of them also opposed the referendum. They objected to perfected commonwealth as an option in the election since it was a term without any certain meaning. No one knew how far Congress would go toward a perfected commonwealth and no one would know until after the election was over.

The old line PER leadership opposed the election. One group, led by Luis Ferré, felt that the time had come to settle things. They also believed that Muñoz Marín was slipping in power and that they had a chance of winning the election. The *independentistas* refused to participate in the election.

Muñoz Marín and Ferré campaigned throughout the island, but the vote in the summer of 1967 was not even close. Two-thirds of the people turned out to vote (a high turnout for most elections, a low turnout for a matter this crucial), and 61 percent favored the commonwealth option while 39 percent favored statehood.

It is fair to ask how fair the election was. Muñoz Marín was a figure of towering popularity, especially in the rural areas of Puerto Rico. The statehood supporters had no one of equal stature. The perfected commonwealth was an undefined idea. No one knew what problems might arise from it, but people did know that statehood presented economic and cultural problems. They were worried about federal taxes and imposition of English as an official language. So the contest was between an idea whose problems were unknown and one whose problems were known.

The meaning of the election can be debated forever. Indeed, in Puerto Rico it has been debated for over twenty years. Muñoz Marín proclaimed it a victory for the idea of a permanent, perfected commonwealth and that the status issue was settled forever. If he believed that, he was alone.

For many people, the referendum seemed a victory for the statehood supporters, for they had done well in voting that seemed to be rigged against them. Indeed, the very next year saw the rise of a new prostatehood political party, the New Progressive party (PNP), headed by Luis Ferré.

Ferré was in many ways the opposite of Muñoz Marín. He was of French descent, not Spanish. He did not engage in political activity until he was nearly fifty. He was a very wealthy industrialist whose family had been involved in business in Puerto Rico since the end of World War I. His training was not in the liberal arts, but in mechanical and electrical engineering. He had degrees in both from the Massachusetts Institute of Technology.

In its first election, the PNP took the governorship and control of one house of the legislature away from the PPD. So in one year, the people of Puerto Rico had voted strongly for commonwealth status. The next year they had voted, though very narrowly, for a prostatehood government. However, Ferré's election in 1968 was not entirely based on his position regarding statehood. Ferré's New Progressive party had split off from the Republican Statehood party. Muñoz Marín's Popular Democratic party had split also. The governor, Roberto Sanchez Vilella, a member of the PPD, had divorced and remarried during his term in office. Such actions were very unpopular in this heavily Catholic island, and he was dropped as candidate for reelection and replaced by Luis Negron Lopez. Sanchez Vilella started his own party and ran for governor as well. So there were four candidates in the election of 1968. Ferré's election as the first governor who was not a member of the PPD was a bit of a fluke, then. But his election also made it very clear that the status issue had not been resolved at all.

In fact, the issue seemed more polarizing than ever. In 1972, the PPD won back the governorship. In 1976, the PNP took it back again and kept it in 1980. In 1984, the PPD once more took control.

The more radical *independentistas* were increasingly removed from the political process. There was very little

political support for the concept of immediate independence and not much more for a gradual independence.
Some *independentistas* became increasingly violent. Their
violence, unfortunately, was responded to in some in-
stances by illegal violence on the part of law enforcment
authorities. In the early 1980s, two young *independentistas*
were killed by police in an incident that many believe to
have been a trap. The incident, called *Cerro Maravilla* for
the hilltop on which it took place, led to an investigation
that made the Watergate investigation in the continental
United States look like a polite and quiet inquiry. The
entire island was glued to its television sets for months,
and every newspaper filled its front pages with accounts
of the investigation. Puerto Ricans love political drama,
and this incident, tragic and unfortunate as it was,
brought political drama of the most intense sort. It also
led to the downfall of the PNP governor, Carlos Romero
Barceló, in 1984.

Romero was replaced by the man he had replaced,
Rafael Hernández Colón. Hernández Colón served as
governor from 1972 to 1976. He was elected again in 1984
and then reelected in 1988. When first elected, he was
only thirty-six years old. He is the son of a former justice
of the Supreme Court of Puerto Rico. A lawyer, he went
to college at Johns Hopkins University in the United
States and then attended the University of Puerto Rico
School of Law. In 1965, at age twenty-nine, he became
attorney general of Puerto Rico.

After the 1968 elections, in which the PNP won its first
election, Hernández Colón found himself in a PPD that

had no obvious leader. He stepped into the gap, and by the end of 1969 he was both president of the senate, to which he had just been elected for the first time, and president of the PPD. He received Muñoz Marín's strong personal backing and was elected governor in 1972 by a clear but slim majority of votes. His elections in 1984 and 1988 were also fairly close.

The society was polarized between two choices, and no significant and permanent majority favored either one. This polarization had, and continues to have, enormously damaging effects in Puerto Rico. When the central issue is political status, the other issues take second place. In a place where 25 percent of the population is out of work and where health care needs and educational needs are great, such a result is tragic.

It has not helped matters greatly that the issue is even more confusing to Americans than it is to Puerto Ricans. Few Americans realize that while Puerto Ricans pay extremely high local taxes, they pay no federal taxes. Statehood, then, means the imposition of a higher tax rate. Few Americans realize that Puerto Rico is eligible for some federal programs and ineligible for others in no logical pattern. Statehood would mean inclusion in all federal programs.

It is fair to assume, although it is hotly disputed, that Congress would not permit statehood without a requirement that English be an official language of Puerto Rico—or perhaps the only language. Yet such a condition would be unacceptable to a great many Puerto Ricans. Independence, on the other hand, would mean that

Puerto Rico would lose its tariff-free trading status with the United States. The United States is not free to give one nation a lower tariff rate than others. It has treaties with nations all over the world that give them what is called "most favored nation" status. That means that those countries can trade with the United States on the same basis as the nation with the most favorable arrangement with the United States. As a commonwealth, Puerto Rico's trade arrangements with the United States are more favorable than those of any foreign nation. If those arrangements were to remain after Puerto Rico was to become independent, then many other nations would be entitled to the same level of treatment, and that would be extremely expensive for the United States, so it is not likely to happen.

Given these difficulties, and there are others, no change in status can come without significant loss. At the same time, the issue remains a constant distraction, and it must somehow, at long last, be resolved in a manner that is accepted as a long-term solution.

In 1978, President Carter called for a new referendum on the issue, although it also appears that he was concerned about an upcoming United Nations vote accusing the United States of colonialism in Puerto Rico. The referendum never took place.

In January of 1989, the leaders of the three major political groups in Puerto Rico all called for a new referendum on the status issue. Such agreements have been short-lived in Puerto Rican history. Nonetheless, almost everyone would agree that the issue should be settled.

In his first speech to Congress in February of 1989, President Bush supported that call for a referendum. But the problems that made the 1967 referendum effectively meaningless remain. No one has a clear idea of what a permanent commonwealth would be like. No one has a clear idea of how the United States would regard Puerto Rico if it were independent. No one has a clear idea of whether Congress would require federal taxes and an official English language if Puerto Rico were to become a state. Until those problems are resolved, until people can know with some degree of certainty what a change in status would involve, there is no meaning to a referendum vote. The outcome of such a vote would be disputed for another twenty years, unless the vote was on three separate plans that included some level of specifics. In debating the proposal for a new referendum, Congress seemed to be ready to include some of the specifics.

The hard choices in the days and the years ahead must be made by Puerto Ricans. But their decisions will be greatly effected by decisions made in the United States. Those American decisions will be better decisions if they are well-informed ones.

Even if the proposed referendum is held, it is likely that Puerto Rico will "belong" to the United States without being "a part of the United States" for many years to come. Even if someday Puerto Ricans choose independence, Puerto Rico's closeness to the United States, and the fact that millions of people in the United States have Puerto Rican ancestors, mean that there will be a close and special relationship. The culture of Puerto Rico is a century older than the culture of any other part of the United States. It is a basically Spanish culture. Moreover, as an island with a population that shares a common ethnic and religious heritage, its culture is particularly strong. It has not had to adapt to other cultures, as have most areas of the United States. This gives it a depth and strength that is hard to understand until you have seen it firsthand. It makes Puerto Rico a special place in the New World and one from which all Americans can learn a great deal.

# Bibliography

*There are very few books in English on Puerto Rico. Most of* them are very hard to get, either because they are out of print or because they are books of largely academic interest. Even in an academic bookstore, they are hard to find on the shelves. Some such stores will include them in American history. Others will classify them as Latin American. Every now and then, a store will have a Caribbean section, and the books will be placed there. Even bookstore owners are confused about the status of Puerto Rico. Books on American history basically ignore Puerto Rico. Probably the most widely used college American history text refers to Puerto Rico twice. The first time it refers to Puerto Rico when it was taken during the Spanish-American War, the second time when the commonwealth was established.

There are two recent books, both available in paperback, that can be recommended for students, but only as research aids. They are both serious academic efforts and they are sometimes rather slow reading because of the enormous detail they include. These are the two:

Carr, Raymond. *Puerto Rico: A Colonial Experiment.* New York: Vintage, 1984. An Oxford professor examines objectively the relationship between Puerto Rico and the United States. Contains a brief history of the precommonwealth period that is quite readable.

Morales Carrion, Arturo, ed. *Puerto Rico: A Political and Cultural History.* New York: Norton, 1983. By far the most comprehensive book on the subject in recent years. A team of distinguished scholars from Puerto Rico examines the entire history in a chronological way. Statehooders will probably argue that the book is biased against their position, and they are probably right, but as a one-volume summary of the past of Puerto Rico, it has no equal in English.

Another book is unfortunately rather far out-of-date and out of print as well.

Lewis, Gordon. *Puerto Rico: Freedom and Power in the Caribbean.* New York: Monthly Review (MR) Press, 1963. This book may be found, as mine was, in a secondhand bookstore. Its sections on the early history are clear and concise and its viewpoint fairly objective.

The following books may also be of interest. Some of these are either biased or very biased. People feel very strongly about political questions in Puerto Rico. Objective analysis is hard to find. But reading different books with different biases is one way of forming your own views.

Babin, Maria Teresa, and Stan Borinquen Steiner, eds. *An Anthology of Puerto Rican Literature.* New York: Vintage Books, 1974.

Lewis, Oscar. *La Vida.* New York: Random House, 1965. An anthropologist's comparison of Puerto Rican life in San Juan and New York.

Lopez, Alfredo. *Dona Licha's Island: Modern Colonialism in Puerto Rico.* Boston: South End Press, 1987.

Tugwell, Rexford. *The Stricken Land.* New York: Doubleday, 1947.

Wagneheim, Kal. *Puerto Rico: A Profile.* New York: Praeger, 1970.

There are no English biographies in print of any historical figures from Puerto Rico. Biographies of Muñoz Marín and Muñoz Rivera can be found in some encyclopedias. A biography of Muñoz Marín from 1953 can be found in that year's volume of *Current Biography.* That series also includes biographies of Rafael Hernández Colón (1973) and Luis Ferré (1970). An out-of-print biography of Luis Muñoz Marín that does not cover his later years is the following:

Aitken, Thomas. *Poet in the Forest: The Story of Luis Muñoz Marín.* New York: University of Puerto Rico Press, 1964.

Some general background on Latin American history may also be useful and interesting. Three good and readily available books are these:

Pendle, George. *A History of Latin America.* (Pelican, 1976).

Williams, Eric. *From Columbus to Castro: The History of the Caribbean.* New York: Vintage Books, 1984.

Worcester, Donald and Wendell Schaeffer. *The Growth and Culture of Latin America.* Oxford: Oxford University Press.

The second of these books is by Eric Williams, who for twenty years was the prime minister of Trinidad and Tobago. Williams focuses on the issue of slavery in the Caribbean colonies and economic factors in the postcolonial period. The book has not been updated since 1970, but it is very well written and very full in its coverage.

# Index

*129*

**Henry Waldinger Memorial Library**

Valley Stream, New York

Phone: VA 5-6422

PLEASE LEAVE CARD
IN POCKET

VS